The Complete
Grimm's
Fairy Tales

Jacob Grimm and Wilhelm Grimm

Pacific Publishing Studio

Published in the United States by Madison Park, an imprint of Pacific Publishing Studio.

www.PacPS.com

ISBN1453697284

EAN-139781453697283

Special acknowledgement is made to the following:

Transcription: Pacific Publishing Studio

The Complete

Grimm's

Fairy Tales

Table of Contents

The Frog Prince

A **LONG TIME AGO,** when wishes could still come true, there lived a king whose daughters were all beautiful. The youngest was so beautiful that the sun itself, which has seen so much, was astonished whenever it shone in her face. Close by the King's castle was a great dark forest, and under an old lime-tree in the forest was a well, and when the day was very warm the King's child went out into the forest and sat down by the side of the cool fountain. And when she was bored she took a golden ball and threw it up high and caught it. And this ball was her favorite plaything.

Now it so happened that on one occasion the princess's golden ball did not fall into the little hand which she was holding up for it, but onto the ground beyond, and rolled straight into the water. The King's daughter followed it with her eyes, but it vanished, and the well was deep so deep that the bottom could not be seen. On this she began to cry. She cried louder and louder and could not be comforted. And as she sat sulking someone said to her, "What ails you, King's daughter? You look so sad that even a stone would feel pity for you."

She looked round to the side from whence the voice came and saw a frog stretching its thick, ugly head from the water. "Ah! old water-splasher, is that you?" she said; "I am weeping for my golden ball, which has fallen into the well."

"Be quiet and do not weep," answered the frog, "I can help you, but what will you give me if I bring your ball out of the well?"

"Whatever you want, dear frog," she said. "My clothes, my pearls and jewels, and even the golden crown that I am wearing."

The frog answered, "I do not care for your clothes, your pearls and jewels, or your golden crown. But if you will love me and let me be your companion and playmate, and sit by you at your little table, and eat off your little golden plate, and drink out of your little cup, and sleep in your little bed—if you will promise me this, I will go down below and bring your golden ball up again."

"Oh yes," she said, "I promise you all that you wish, if you will bring me my ball back again." She thought, "How the silly frog does talk! He lives in the water with the other frogs, and croaks, and can be no companion to any human being!"

But the frog, when he had received this promise, put his head into the water and sank down, and in a short while came swimming up again with the ball in his mouth and threw it on the grass. The King's daughter was delighted to see her pretty plaything once more, and picked it up, and ran away with it. "Wait, wait," said the frog. "Take me with you. I can't run as fast as you can." But what did it avail him to scream his croak, croak, after her, as loudly as he could? She did not listen to it, but ran home and soon forgot the poor frog, who was forced to go back into his well again.

The next day when she had seated herself at table with the King and all the courtiers, and was eating from her little golden plate, something came creeping splish splash, splish splash, up the marble staircase, and when it had got to the top, it knocked at the door and cried, "Princess, youngest princess, open the door for me." She ran to see who was outside, but when she opened the door, there sat the frog in front of it. Then she slammed the door closed, in great haste, sat down to dinner again, and was quite frightened.

The King saw plainly that her heart was beating violently, and said, "My child, what are you so afraid of? Is there a giant outside who wants to carry you away?"

"Ah, no," replied she. "It is no giant but a disgusting frog."

"What does a frog want with you?"

"Ah, dear father, yesterday when I was in the forest sitting by the well and playing, my golden ball fell into the water. And because I cried, the frog brought it out again for me, and because he insisted, I promised him he should be my companion, but I never thought he would be able to come out of his water! And now he is outside there and wants to come in to see me."

In the meantime it knocked a second time, and cried, "Princess! Youngest princess! Open the door for me! Do you not know what you said to me yesterday by the cool waters of the fountain? Princess, youngest princess! Open the door for me!"

It was then that the King said, "That which you have promised you must perform. Go and let him in."

She went and opened the door, and the frog hopped in and followed her, step by step, to her chair. There he sat and cried, "Lift me up beside you." She delayed, until at last the King commanded her to do it. When the frog was once on the chair he wanted to be on the table, and when he was on the table he said, "Now, push your little golden plate nearer to me so that we may eat together."

She did this, but it was easy to see that she did not do it willingly. The frog enjoyed what he ate, but almost every mouthful she took choked her. At length he said, "I have eaten and am satisfied; now I am tired, carry me into your little room and make your little silken bed ready, and we will both lie down and go to sleep."

The King's daughter began to cry, for she was afraid of the cold frog which she did not like to touch, and which was now to sleep in her pretty, clean little bed. But the King grew angry and said, "He who helped you when you were in trouble ought not afterwards to be despised by you." So she took hold of the frog with two fingers, carried him upstairs, and put him in a corner. But when she was in bed he crept to her and said, "I am tired, I want to sleep as well as you, lift me up or I will tell your father."

This made her terribly angry and she took him up and threw him with all her might against the wall. "Now, you will be quiet, odious frog," she said. But when he fell down, he was no frog but a King's son with beautiful kind eyes. He, by her father's will, was now her dear companion and husband. Then he told her how he had been bewitched by a wicked witch, and how no one could have delivered him from the well but herself, and that tomorrow they would go together into his kingdom.

Then they went to sleep, and next morning when the sun awoke them, a carriage came driving up with eight white horses, which had white ostrich feathers on their heads and were harnessed with golden chains, and behind stood the young King's servant Faithful Henry. Faithful Henry had been so unhappy when his master was changed into a frog that he had caused three iron bands to be laid round his heart, so that it would not burst with grief and sadness.

The carriage was to conduct the young King into his Kingdom. Faithful Henry helped them both in and placed himself behind again, and was full of joy because of this deliverance. And when they had driven a part of the way the King's son heard a cracking behind him as if something had broken. So he turned round and cried, "Henry, the carriage is breaking."

"No, master, it is not the carriage. It is a band from my heart, which was put there in my great pain when you were a frog and imprisoned in the well."

Again and once again while they were on their way something cracked, and each time the King's son thought the carriage was breaking; but it was only the bands which were springing from the heart of faithful Henry because his master was set free and was happy.

Cat and Mouse

⌘

ONCE UPON A TIME, a cat made friends with a mouse, and had said so much to her about the great love and friendship she felt for her, that at length the mouse agreed that they should live and keep house together. "But we must make a provision for winter, or else we will suffer from hunger," said the cat, "and you, little mouse, cannot venture everywhere, or you will be caught in a trap some day."

The good advice was followed, and a pot of fat was bought, but they did not know where to put it. At length, after much consideration, the cat said, "I know no place where it will be better stored up than in the church, for no one dares take anything away from there. We will set it beneath the altar, and not touch it until we are really in need of it."

So the pot was placed in safety, but it was not long before the cat had a great yearning for it, and said to the mouse, "I want to tell you something, little mouse; my cousin has brought a little son into the world, and has asked me to be godmother; he is white with brown spots, and I am to hold him over the font at the christening. Let me go out today, and you look after the house by yourself."

"Yes, yes," answered the mouse, "by all means go, and if you get anything very good, think of me, I should like a drop of sweet red christening wine too."

All this, however, was untrue; the cat had no cousin, and had not been asked to be godmother. She went straight to the church, stole to the pot of fat, began to lick at it, and licked the top of the fat off. Then she took a walk upon the roofs of the town, looked out for opportunities, and then stretched herself in the sun, and licked her lips whenever she thought of the pot of fat, and not until it was evening did she return home. "Well, here you are again," said the mouse, "no doubt you have had a merry day." "All went off well," answered the cat. "What name did they give the child?"

"Top off!" said the cat quite coolly.

"Top off!" cried the mouse, "that is a very odd and uncommon name, is it a usual one in your family?"

"What does it signify," said the cat, "it is no worse than crumb-stealer, as your god-children are called."

Before long the cat was seized by another fit of longing. She said to the mouse, "You must do me a favor, and once more manage the house for a day alone. I am again asked to be godmother, and, as the child has a white ring round its neck, I cannot refuse."

The good mouse consented, but the cat crept behind the town walls to the church, and devoured half the pot of fat. "Nothing ever seems so good as what one keeps to oneself," she said, and was quite satisfied with her day's work.

When she went home the mouse inquired, "And what was this child christened?"

"Half-done," answered the cat. "Half-done! What are you saying? I never heard the name in my life, I'll wager anything it is not in the calendar!"

The cat's mouth soon began to water for some more licking. "All good things go in threes," she said, "I am asked to stand godmother again. The child is quite black, only it has white paws, but with that exception, it has not a single white hair on its whole body; this only happens once every few years, you will let me go, won't you?"

"Top-off! Half-done!" answered the mouse, "they are such odd names, they make me very thoughtful."

"You sit at home," said the cat, "in your dark-grey fur coat and long tail, and are filled with fancies, that's because you do not go out in the daytime."

During the cat's absence the mouse cleaned the house and put it in order, but the greedy cat entirely emptied the pot of fat. "When everything is eaten up one has some peace," she said to herself, and well filled and fat she did not return home till night. The mouse at once asked what name had been given to the third child.

"It will not please you more than the others," said the cat. "He is called All-gone."

"All-gone," cried the mouse, "that is the most suspicious name of all! I have never seen it in print. All gone; what can that mean?" And she shook her head, curled herself up, and lay down to sleep.

From this time forth no one invited the cat to be godmother, but when the winter had come and there was no longer anything to be found outside, the mouse thought of their provision, and said, "Come cat, we will go to our pot of fat which we have stored up for ourselves—we will enjoy that."

"Yes," answered the cat, "you will enjoy it as much as you would enjoy sticking that dainty tongue of yours out of the window." They set out on their way, but when they arrived, the pot of fat certainly was still in its place, but it was empty.

"Alas," said the mouse, "now I see what has happened. Now it comes to light! You are a true friend! You have devoured all when you were standing godmother. First top off, then half done, then..."

"Will you hold your tongue," cried the cat, "one word more and I will eat you too."

"All gone" was already on the poor mouse's lips; scarcely had she spoken it before the cat sprang on her, seized her, and swallowed her down. Verily, that is the way of the world.

Mary's Child

✡

ONCE UPON A TIME, a wood cutter and his wife lived near a great forest. The couple had an only child, a little girl three years old. They were so poor, however, that they no longer had daily bread and did not know how to get food for her. One morning the wood-cutter went out sorrowfully to his work in the forest, and while he was cutting wood, suddenly there stood before him a tall and beautiful woman with a crown of shining stars on her head, who said to him, "I am the Virgin Mary, mother of the child Jesus. You are poor and needy, bring your child to me. I will take her with me and be her mother and care for her."

The wood-cutter obeyed, brought his child, and gave her to the Virgin Mary, who took her up to heaven with her. There the child fared well, ate sugar-cakes, and drank sweet milk, and her clothes were of gold, and the little angels played with her. And when she was fourteen years of age, the Virgin Mary called her one day and said, "Dear child, I am about to make a long journey, so take into your keeping the keys of the thirteen doors of heaven. Twelve of these you may open, and behold the glory which is within them, but the thirteenth, to which this little key belongs, is forbidden to you. Beware of opening it, or you will bring misery on yourself."

The girl promised to be obedient, and when the Virgin Mary was gone, she began to examine the dwellings of the kingdom of heaven. Each day she opened one of them, until she had seen all twelve. In each of them sat one of the Apostles in the midst of a great light, and she rejoiced in all the magnificence and splendor; and the little angels who always accompanied her rejoiced with her.

Then the forbidden door alone remained, and she felt a great desire to know what could be hidden behind it, and said to the angels, "I will not quite open it, and I will not go inside it, but I will unlock it so that we can just see a little through the opening."

"Oh no," said the little angels, "that would be a sin. The Virgin Mary has forbidden it, and it might easily cause you unhappiness."

Then she was silent, but the desire in her heart was not stilled, but gnawed there and tormented her, and let her have no rest. And once when the angels had all gone out, she thought, "Now I am quite alone, and I could peep in. If I do it, no one will ever know."

She sought out the key, and when she had got it in her hand, she put it in the lock, and when she had put it in, she turned it round as well. Then the door sprang open, and she saw there the Trinity sitting in fire and splendor. She stayed there awhile, and looked at everything in amazement. Then she touched the light a little with her finger, and her finger became quite golden. Immediately a great fear fell on her. She shut the door violently and ran away. Her terror too would not cease, no matter what she did, and her heart beat continually and would not be still. The gold too stayed on her finger and would not go away, even as she rubbed it and washed it ever so much.

It was not long before the Virgin Mary came back from her journey. She called the girl before her, and asked to have the keys of heaven back. When the maiden gave her the bunch, the Virgin looked into her eyes and said, "Did you open the thirteenth door also?"

"No," she replied. Then she laid her hand on the girl's heart, and felt how it beat and beat, and saw right well that she had disobeyed her order and had opened the door. Then she said once again, "Are you certain that you have not done it?"

"Yes," said the girl, for the second time. Then she saw the finger, which had become golden from touching the fire of heaven, and saw well that the child had sinned, and said for the third time, "Have you not done it?"

"No," said the girl for the third time.

Then said the Virgin Mary, "You have not obeyed me, and besides that you have lied, you are no longer worthy to be in heaven."

Then the girl fell into a deep sleep, and when she awoke she lay on the earth below, in the midst of a wilderness. She wanted to cry out, but she could bring forth no sound. She sprang up and wanted to run away, but which ever direction she turned herself, she was continually held back by thick hedges of thorns through which she could not break.

In the desert, in which she was imprisoned, there stood an old hollow tree, and this had to be her dwelling-place. Into this she crept when night came, and here she slept. Here, too, she found a shelter from storm and rain, but it was a miserable life, and bitterly did she weep when she remembered how happy she had been in heaven, and how the angels had played with her.

Roots and wild berries were her only food, and for these she sought as far as she could go. In the autumn, she picked up the fallen nuts and leaves and carried them into the hole. The nuts were her food in winter, and when snow and ice came, she crept amongst the leaves like a poor little animal so that she would not freeze.

Before long her clothes were all torn and one bit of them after another fell off her. As soon, however, as the sun shone warm again, she went out and sat in front of the tree, and her long hair covered her on all sides like a mantle. Here she sat year after year, and felt the pain and the misery of the world.

One day, when the trees were once more clothed in fresh green, the King of the country was hunting in the forest, and followed a roe, and as it had fled into the thicket that shut in this part of the forest, he got off his horse, tore through the bushes, and cut himself a path with his sword. When he had at last forced his way through, he saw a wonderfully beautiful maiden sitting under the tree. She sat there and was entirely covered with her golden hair down to her very feet. He stood still and looked at her full of surprise, then he spoke to her and said, "Who are you? Why are you sitting here in the wilderness?"

But she gave no answer, for she could not open her mouth. The King continued, "Wilt you go with me to my castle?"

Then she just nodded her head a little. The King took her in his arms, carried her to his horse, and rode home with her. When he reached the royal castle, he had her dressed in beautiful garments and gave her all things in abundance. Although she could not speak, she was still so beautiful and charming that he began to love her with all his heart, and it was not long before he married her.

After a year or so had passed, the Queen had a baby boy. At this time, the Virgin Mary appeared to her in the night when she lay in her bed alone, and said, "If you will tell the truth and confess that you unlocked the forbidden door, I will open your mouth and give you back your speech. But if you lie and deny the truth, I will take your new-born child away with me."

Then the queen was permitted to answer, but she remained hard, and said, "No, I did not open the forbidden door;" and the Virgin Mary took the new-born child from her arms, and vanished with it.

The next morning when the child was not to be found, it was whispered among the people that the Queen was a man-eater, and had killed her own child. She heard all this and could say nothing to the contrary, but the King would not believe it, for he loved her so much.

When a year had gone by, the Queen had another baby boy, and in the night the Virgin Mary again came to her and said, "If you will confess that you opened the forbidden door, I will give your child back and untie you tongue; but if you continue in sin and deny it, I will take away with me this new child also."

Then the Queen again said, "No, I did not open the forbidden door;" and the Virgin took the child out of her arms, and away with her to heaven.

Next morning, when this child also had disappeared, the people declared quite loudly that the Queen had devoured it, and the King's councilors demanded that she should be brought to justice. The King, however, loved her so dearly that he would not believe it, and commanded the councilors under pain of death not to say any more about it.

The following year, the Queen gave birth to a beautiful little daughter, and for the third time, the Virgin Mary appeared to her in the night and said, "Follow me."

She took the Queen by the hand and led her to heaven, and showed her there her two eldest children, who smiled at her, and were playing with the ball of the world. When the Queen rejoiced at the site of her two children, the Virgin Mary said, "Is your heart not yet softened? If you will admit that you opened the forbidden door, I will give you back your two little sons."

But for the third time the Queen answered, "No, I did not open the forbidden door." Then the Virgin let her sink down to earth once more and took from her likewise her third child.

Next morning, when the loss was reported abroad, all the people cried loudly, "The Queen is a man-eater. She must be judged," and the King was no longer able to restrain his councilors. Thereupon a trial was held, and as she could not answer, and defend herself, she was condemned to be burned alive.

The wood was gathered, and when she was tied to the stake, and the fire began to burn round about her, the hard ice of pride melted, her heart was moved by repentance, and she thought, "If I could but confess before my death that I opened the door."

Then her voice came back to her, and she cried out loudly, "Yes, Mary, I did it." Immediately rain fell from the sky and extinguished the flames of fire, and a light broke out above her, and the Virgin Mary descended with the two little sons by her side, and the newborn daughter in her arms. She spoke kindly to her, and said, "She who repents her sin and acknowledges it, is forgiven."

Then she gave her the three children, untied her tongue, and granted her happiness for her whole life.

Rapunzel

✂

ONCE UPON A TIME, there was man and a woman who had long in vain wished for a child. At length the woman hoped that God was about to grant her desire. These people had a little window at the back of their house from which a splendid garden could be seen, which was full of the most beautiful flowers and herbs. It was, however, surrounded by a high wall, and no one dared to go into it because it belonged to an enchantress, who had great power and was dreaded by all the world.

One day the woman was standing by this window and looking down into the garden, when she saw a bed which was planted with the most beautiful rapunzel, and it looked so fresh and green that she longed for it, and had the greatest desire to eat some. This desire increased every day, and as she knew that she could not get any of it, she quite pined away, and looked pale and miserable.

Then her husband was alarmed, and asked, "What is wrong, dear wife?"

"Ah," she replied, "if I can't get some of the rapunzel that is in the garden behind our house, to eat, I will die."

The man, who loved her, thought, "Sooner than let my wife die, I will bring her some of the rapunzel myself. Let it cost me what it will."

In the twilight of the evening, he clambered down over the wall into the garden of the enchantress, hastily clutched a handful of rapunzel, and took it to his wife. She at once made herself a salad of it, and ate it with much relish. She, however, liked it so much—so very much, that the next day she longed for it three times as much as before. If he was to have any rest, her husband must once more descend into the garden.

In the gloom of evening, he let himself down again; but when he had clambered down the wall he was terribly afraid, for he saw the enchantress standing before him.

"How can you dare," she said with angry look, "descend into my garden and steal my rapunzel like a thief? You will suffer for it!"

"Ah," he answered, "let mercy take the place of justice, I only made up my mind to do it out of necessity. My wife saw your rapunzel from the window, and felt such a longing for it that she would have died if she had not got some to eat."

Then the enchantress allowed her anger to be softened, and said to him, "If the case be as you said, I will allow you to take as much rapunzel as you want, only I make one condition: you must give me the child which your wife will bring into the world. It will be well treated, and I will care for it like a mother."

The man in his terror consented to everything, and when the woman gave birth, the enchantress appeared at once, gave the child the name of Rapunzel, and took it away with her.

Rapunzel grew into the most beautiful child beneath the sun. When she was twelve years old, the enchantress shut her into a tower, which lay in a forest, and had neither stairs nor door, but right at the top was a little window. When the enchantress wanted to go in, she placed herself beneath it and cried, "Rapunzel, Rapunzel, let down your hair to me."

Rapunzel had magnificent long hair, fine as spun gold, and when she heard the voice of the enchantress, she unfastened her braided tresses, wound them round one of the hooks of the window above, and then the hair fell seven stories down, and the enchantress climbed up it.

After a year or two, it came to pass that the King's son rode through the forest and went by the tower. Then he heard a song, which was so charming that he stood still and listened. This was Rapunzel, who in her solitude passed her time in letting her sweet voice resound. The King's son wanted to climb up to her. He looked for the door of the tower, but none was to be found. He rode home, but the singing had so deeply touched his heart, that every day he went out into the forest and listened to it. Once, when he was standing behind a tree, he saw that an enchantress came there and he heard how she cried, "Rapunzel, Rapunzel, let down your hair."

Then Rapunzel let down the braids of her hair, and the enchantress climbed up to her.

"If that is the ladder by which one mounts, I will for once try my fortune," he said. And the next day when it began to grow dark, he went to the tower and cried, "Rapunzel, Rapunzel, let down your hair."

Immediately, the hair fell down and the King's son climbed up.

At first Rapunzel was terribly frightened when a man she had never seen before came to her; but the King's son began to talk to her quite like a friend, and told her that his heart had been so stirred that it had let him have no rest, and he had been forced to see her.

Then Rapunzel lost her fear, and when he asked her if she would take him for her husband, and she saw that he was young and handsome, she thought, "He will love me more than old Dame Gothel does," and she said yes, and laid her hand in his.

She said, "I will willingly go away with you, but I do not know how to get down. Bring with you a spool of silk every time you come, and I will weave a ladder with it, and when that is ready I will descend, and you will take me on your horse."

They agreed that until that time he should come to her every evening, for the old woman came by day. The enchantress remarked nothing of this, until once Rapunzel said to her, "Tell me, Dame Gothel, how it happens that you are so much heavier for me to draw up than the young King's son—he is with me in a moment."

"Ah! You wicked child," cried the enchantress. "What did I hear you say? I thought I had separated you from all the world, and yet you have deceived me. In her anger she clutched Rapunzel's beautiful tresses, wrapped them twice round her left hand, seized a pair of scissors with the right, and snip, snap, they were cut off, and the lovely braids lay on the ground. And she was so pitiless that she took poor Rapunzel into a desert where she had to live in grief and misery.

On the same day, however, that she cast out Rapunzel, the enchantress fastened the braids of hair, which she had cut off, to the hook of the window, and when the King's son came and cried, "Rapunzel, Rapunzel, let down your hair," she let the hair down.

The King's son ascended, but he did not find his dearest Rapunzel above, but the enchantress, who gazed at him with wicked and venomous looks.

"Aha!" she cried mockingly, "You came for your dearest, but the beautiful bird sits no longer singing in the nest; the cat has got it, and will scratch out your eyes as well. Rapunzel is lost to you; you will never see her again."

The King's son was beside himself with pain, and in his despair he leapt down from the tower. He escaped with his life, but the thorns into which he fell, pierced his eyes. Then he wandered quite blind about the forest, ate nothing but roots and berries, and did nothing but lament and weep over the loss of his dearest wife. Thus he roamed about in misery for some years, and at length came to the desert where Rapunzel, with the twins to which she had given birth, a boy and a girl, lived in wretchedness.

He heard a voice, and it seemed so familiar to him that he went towards it, and when he approached, Rapunzel knew him and fell on his neck and wept. Two of her tears wetted his eyes and they grew clear again, and he could see with them as before. He led her to his kingdom where he was joyfully received, and they lived for a long time afterwards, happy and contented.

Hansel and Gretel

☾

NEXT TO A GREAT FOREST lived a poor wood-cutter with his wife and two children. The boy was called Hansel and the girl Gretel. He had little to eat and to break, and eventually when things food and wood became very scarce, he could no longer make daily bread. Now when he thought over this by night in his bed, and tossed about in his anxiety, he groaned and said to his wife, who was the step-mother of his children, "What is to become of us? How are we to feed our poor children, when we no longer have anything even for ourselves?"

"I'll tell you what, husband," answered the step-mother, "early tomorrow morning we will take the children out into the forest to where it is the thickest, there we will light a fire for them, and give each of them one piece of bread more, and then we will go to our work and leave them alone. They will not find the way home again, and we will be rid of them."

"No," said the man, "I will not do that; how can I bear to leave my children alone in the forest? The wild animals would soon come and tear them to pieces."

"O, you fool!" she said, "Then we will all four die of hunger. You may as well plane the planks for our coffins," and she left him no peace until he consented.

"But I feel very sorry for the poor children, all the same," said the man.

The two children had also not been able to sleep for hunger, and had heard what their step-mother had said to their father. Gretel wept bitter tears, and said to Hansel, "Now all is over with us."

"Be quiet, Gretel," said Hansel, "do not worry, I will soon find a way to help us."

And when the old folks had fallen asleep, he got up, put on his little coat, opened the door below, and crept outside. The moon shone brightly, and the white pebbles which lay in front of the house glittered like real silver pennies. Hansel stooped and put as many of them in the little pocket of his coat as he could possibly get in. Then he went back and said to Gretel, "Be comforted, dear little sister, and sleep in peace, God will not forsake us," and he lay down again in his bed.

When day dawned, but before the sun had risen, the woman came and awoke the two children, saying "Get up, you sluggards! We are going into the forest to fetch wood."

She gave each a little piece of bread, and said, "There is something for your dinner, but do not eat it up before then, for you will get nothing else."

Gretel took the bread under her apron, as Hansel hid the stones in his pocket. Then they all set out together on the way to the forest. When they had walked a short time, Hansel stood still and peeped back at the house, and did so again and again. His father said, "Hansel, what are you looking at there and staying behind for? Pay attention, and try to keep up."

"Ah, father," said Hansel, "I am looking at my little white cat, which is sitting up on the roof and wants to say good-bye to me."

The wife said, "Fool, that is not your little cat, that is the morning sun which is shining on the chimneys."

Hansel, however, had not been looking back at the cat, but had been constantly throwing one of the white pebble-stones out of his pocket on the road.

When they had reached the middle of the forest, the father said, "Now, children, pile up some wood, and I will light a fire that you may not be cold."

Hansel and Gretel gathered brushwood together, as high as a little hill. The brushwood was lighted, and when the flames were burning very high, the woman said, "Now, children, lay yourselves down by the fire and rest. We will go into the forest and cut some wood. When we are done, we will come back to take you home."

Hansel and Gretel sat by the fire, and when noon came, each ate a little piece of bread, and as they heard the strokes of the wood-axe they believed that their father was near. It was not, however, the axe. It was a branch which he had fastened to a withered tree which the wind was blowing backwards and forwards. And as they had been sitting such a long time, their eyes shut with fatigue, and they fell fast asleep. When at last they awoke, it was already dark night.

Gretel began to cry and said, "How are we to get out of the forest now?"

But Hansel comforted her and said, "Just wait a little, until the moon has risen, and then we will soon find the way." And when the full moon had risen, Hansel took his little sister by the hand, and followed the pebbles, which

The Complete Grimm's Fairy Tales

shone like newly coined silver pieces, and showed them the way.

They walked the whole night long, and by break of day came once more to their father's house. They knocked at the door, and when the woman opened it and saw that it was Hansel and Gretel, she said, "You naughty children, why have you slept so long in the forest? We thought you were never coming back at all!"

The father, however, rejoiced, for it had cut him to the heart to leave them behind alone.

Not long afterwards, there was once more great scarcity in all parts, and the children heard their step-mother saying at night to their father, "Everything is eaten again, we have one half loaf left, and after that there is an end. The children must go. We will take them farther into the wood, so that they will not find their way out again. There is no other means of saving ourselves!"

The man's heart was heavy, and he thought, "it would be better for me to share the last mouthful with my children." The woman, however, would listen to nothing that he had to say, but scolded and reproached him. He who says A must say B, likewise, and as he had yielded the first time, he had to do so a second time also.

The children were, however, still awake and had heard the conversation. When the old folks were asleep, Hansel again got up, and wanted to go out and pick up pebbles as he had done before, but the woman had locked the door, and Hansel could not get out. Nevertheless, he comforted his little sister, and said, "Do not cry, Gretel. Go to sleep quietly. The good God will help us."

Early in the morning came the woman, and took the children out of their beds. Their bit of bread was given to them, but it was smaller than the time before. On the way into the forest, Hansel crumbled his in his pocket, and often stood still and threw a morsel on the ground. "Hansel, why do you stop and look round?" said the father, "Go on."

"I am looking back at my little pigeon which is sitting on the roof, and wants to say good-bye to me," answered Hansel.

"Simpleton!" said the woman, "that is not your little pigeon, that is the morning sun that is shining on the chimney."

Hansel, however, little by little, threw all the crumbs on the path.

The woman led the children still deeper into the forest, where they had never in their lives been before. Then a great fire was again made, and the mother said, "Just sit there, you children, and when you are tired you may sleep a little. We are going into the forest to cut wood, and in the evening when we are done, we will come back to get you."

When it was noon, Gretel shared her piece of bread with Hansel, who had scattered his by the way. Then they fell asleep and evening came and went, but no one came to the poor children. They did not awake until it was dark night, and Hansel comforted his little sister and said, "Just wait, Grethel, until the moon rises, and then we will see the crumbs of bread which I have strewn about. They will show us our way home again."

When the moon came they set out, but they found no crumbs, for the many thousands of birds which fly about in the woods and fields had picked them all up.

Hansel said to Gretel, "We will soon find the way," but they did not find it. They walked the whole night and all the next day too from morning till evening, but they did not get out of the forest, and were very hungry, for they had nothing to eat but two or three berries, which grew on the ground. And as they were so weary that their legs would carry them no longer, they lay down beneath a tree and fell asleep.

It was now three mornings since they had left their father's house. They began to walk again, but they always got deeper into the forest, and if help did not come soon, they would die of hunger and weariness.

When it was mid-day, they saw a beautiful snow-white bird sitting on a bough, which sang so delightfully that they stood still and listened to it. And when it had finished its song, it spread its wings and flew away before them, and they followed it until they reached a little house, on the roof of which it alighted; and when they came up to little house they saw that it was built of bread and covered with cakes, and that the windows were made of clear sugar.

"We will set to work on that," said Hansel, "and have a good meal. I will eat a bit of the roof, and you, Gretel, can eat some of the window; it will taste sweet."

Hansel reached up above, and broke off a little of the roof to try how it tasted, and Gretel leaned against the window and nibbled at the panes.

Then a soft voice cried from the room, "Nibble, nibble, gnaw. Who is nibbling at my little house?"

The children answered, "The wind, the wind, the heaven-born wind," and went on eating without disturbing themselves.

Hansel, who thought the roof tasted very nice, tore down a great piece of it, and Gretel pushed out the whole of one round window-pane, sat down, and enjoyed herself with it.

Suddenly the door opened, and a very, very old woman, who supported herself on crutches, came creeping out. Hansel and Gretel were so terribly frightened that they dropped what they had in their hands.

The old woman, however, nodded her head, and said, "Oh, you dear children, who has brought you here? Do come in and stay with me. No harm will happen to you."

She took them both by the hand, and led them into her little house. Then good food was set before them, milk and pancakes with sugar, apples, and nuts. Afterwards, two pretty little beds were covered with clean white linen, and Hansel and Gretel lay down in them and thought they were in heaven.

The old woman had only pretended to be so kind; she was in reality a wicked witch, who lay in wait for children, and had only built the little house of bread in order to entice them there. When a child fell into her power, she killed it, cooked, and ate it. And that was a feast day for her. Witches have red eyes, and cannot see far, but they have a keen sense of smell like animals, and are aware when human beings draw near. When Hansel and Gretel came into her neighborhood, she laughed maliciously and said mockingly, "I have them, they will not escape me again!"

Early in the morning before the children were awake, she was already up, and when she saw both of them sleeping and looking so pretty, with their plump red cheeks, she muttered to herself, "That will be a dainty mouthful!"

The Complete Grimm's Fairy Tales

Then she seized Hansel with her shriveled hand, carried him into a little stable, and shut him in with a grated door. He screamed all he could, but it was of no use. Then she went to Gretel, shook her till she awoke, and cried, "Get up, lazy thing, fetch some water, and cook something good for your brother. He is in the stable outside and is to be made fat. When he is fat, I will eat him."

Gretel began to weep bitterly, but it was all in vain. She was forced to do what the wicked witch ordered her.

And now the best food was cooked for poor Hansel, but Gretel got nothing but crab-shells. Every morning the woman crept to the little stable, and cried, "Hansel, stretch out your finger so that I may feel if you will soon be fat."

Hansel, however, stretched out a little bone to her, and the old woman, who had dim eyes, could not see it, and thought it was Hansel's finger, and was astonished that there was no way of fattening him. When four weeks had gone by and Hansel still continued thin, she was seized with impatience and would not wait any longer.

"Gretel," she cried to the girl, "be active and bring some water. Whether Hansel is fat or lean, tomorrow I will kill him and cook him."

Ah, how the poor little sister did lament when she had to fetch the water, and how her tears did flow down over her cheeks! "Dear God, do help us," she cried. "If the wild beasts in the forest had but devoured us, we should at any rate have died together."

"Just keep your crying to yourself," said the old woman, "all that won't help you at all."

Early in the morning, Gretel had to go out and hang up the cauldron with the water and light the fire. "We will bake first," said the old woman, "I have already heated the oven and kneaded the dough."

She pushed poor Gretel out to the oven from which flames of fire were already darting. "Creep in," said the witch, "and see if it is properly heated, so that we can bake the bread."

Once Gretel was inside, she intended to shut the oven and let her bake in it, and then she would eat her, too. But Gretel saw what she had in her mind, and said, "I do not know how I am to do it; how do you get in?"

"Silly goose," said the old woman, "The door is big enough. Just look, I can get in myself!" And she crept up and thrust her head into the oven. It was then, that Gretel gave her a push that drove her far into the oven. Gretel shut the iron door and fastened the bolt. Oh! Then the witch began to howl quite horribly, but Gretel ran away and the godless witch was miserably burned to death.

Gretel, however, ran like lightning to Hansel, opened his little stable, and cried, "Hansel, we are saved! The old witch is dead!"

Then Hansel sprang out like a bird from its cage when the door is opened for it. How they did rejoice and embrace each other, and dance about and kiss each other! And as they had no longer any need to fear her, they went into the witch's house, and in every corner there stood chests full of pearls and jewels.

"These are far better than pebbles!" said Hansel, and thrust into his pockets whatever would fit.

Gretel said, "I, too, will take something home with me," and filled her pinafore full.

"But now we will go away," said Hansel, "that we may get out of the witch's forest."

When they had walked for two hours, they came to a great piece of water. "We cannot get over," said Hansel, "I see no foot-plank and no bridge."

"And no boat crosses either," answered Gretel, "but a white duck is swimming there. If I ask her, she will help us over."

Then she cried, "Little duck, little duck, do you see, Hansel and Gretel are waiting for you? There's never a plank or bridge in sight.

Take us across on your back so white."

The duck came to them, and Hansel seated himself on its back, and told his sister to sit by him.

"No," replied Gretel, "that will be too heavy for the little duck. She should take us across, one after the other."

The good little duck did so, and when they were once safely across and had walked for a short time, the forest seemed to be more and more familiar to them, and at length they saw from afar their father's house.

Then they began to run, rushed into the house and threw themselves into their father's arms. The man had not known one happy hour since he had left the children in the forest; the step-mother, however, was dead.

Gretel emptied her pinafore until pearls and precious stones ran about the room, and Hansel threw one handful after another out of his pocket to add to them. Then all anxiety was at an end, and they lived together in perfect happiness.

Cinderella

ONCE UPON A TIME, the wife of a rich man became sick, and as she felt that her end was drawing near, she called her only daughter to her bedside and said, "Dear child, be good and pious, and then the good God will always protect you, and I will look down on you from heaven and be near you."

Thereupon she closed her eyes and departed. Every day the maiden went out to her mother's grave and wept, and she remained pious and good. When winter came, the snow spread a white sheet over the grave, and when the spring sun had drawn it off again, the man had married a new wife.

The woman had brought two daughters into the house with her, who were beautiful and fair of face, but vile and black of heart. Now began a bad time for the poor step-child.

"Is the stupid goose to sit in the parlour with us?" said the mean step-sisters. "She who wants to eat bread must earn it; out with the kitchen-wench."

They took her pretty clothes away from her, put an old grey bedgown on her, and gave her wooden shoes.

"Just look at the proud princess, how decked out she is!" they cried, and laughed, and led her into the kitchen. There she had to do hard work from morning 'til night, get up before daybreak, carry water, light fires, cook, and wash.

Besides this, the sisters did her every imaginable injury. They mocked her and emptied her peas and lentils into the ashes, so that she was forced to sit and pick them out again. In the evening when she had worked until she was weary, she had no bed to go to, but had to sleep by the fireside in the ashes. And because so, she always looked dusty and dirty, they called her Cinderella.

One day, the father was going to the fair, and he asked his two step-daughters what he should bring back for them. "Beautiful dresses," said one, "Pearls and jewels," said the second.

"And you, Cinderella," he said, "what will you have?"

"Father, break off for me the first branch which knocks against your hat on your way home."

So he bought beautiful dresses, pearls, and jewels for his two stepdaughters. And on his way home, as he was riding through a green thicket, a hazel twig brushed against him and knocked off his hat. Then he broke off the branch and took it with him. When he reached home he gave his step-daughters the things that they had wished for, and to Cinderella he gave the branch from the hazel-bush.

Cinderella thanked him, went to her mother's grave and planted the branch on it, and wept so much that the tears fell down on it and watered it. And it grew, however, and became a handsome tree. Three times a day Cinderella went and sat beneath it, and wept and prayed, and a little white bird always came to the tree, and if Cinderella expressed a wish, the bird threw down to her what she had wished for.

It happened, however, that the King appointed a festival which was to last three days, and to which all the beautiful young girls in the country were invited, in order that his son might choose himself a bride. When the two step-sisters heard that they too were to appear among the number, they were delighted, called Cinderella and said, "Comb our hair for us, brush our shoes and fasten our buckles, for we are going to the festival at the King's palace."

Cinderella obeyed, but wept, because she too would have liked to go with them to the dance, and begged her step-mother to allow her to do so.

"You go, Cinderella!" she said; "You are dusty and dirty and would go to the festival? You have no clothes and shoes, and yet would dance!"

Cinderella went on asking, and the stepmother at last said, "I have emptied a dish of lentils into the ashes for you, if you have picked them out again in two hours, you can go with us."

The maiden went through the back-door into the garden and called, "You tame pigeons, you turtle-doves, and all you birds beneath the sky, come and help me to pick the good into the pot, the bad into the crop."

Two white pigeons came in by the kitchen window, and afterwards the turtle-doves, and at last all the birds beneath the sky came whirring and crowding in, and alighted around the ashes. And the pigeons nodded with their heads and began pick, pick, pick, pick, and the rest began also pick, pick, pick, pick, and gathered all the good grains into the dish. Hardly had one hour passed before they had finished, and all flew out again.

Then the girl took the dish to her step-mother and was glad. She believed that now she would be allowed to go with them to the festival. But the step-mother said, "No,

Cinderella, you have no clothes and you cannot dance; you would only be laughed at."

And as Cinderella wept at this, the step-mother said, "If you can pick two dishes of lentils out of the ashes for me in one hour, you can go with us." And she thought to herself, "That, she most certainly cannot do."

When the step-mother had emptied the two dishes of lentils amongst the ashes, Cinderella went through the back-door into the garden and cried, "You tame pigeons, you turtle-doves, and all you birds under heaven, come and help me to pick the good into the pot, the bad into the crop."

Two white pigeons came in by the kitchen window, and afterwards the turtle-doves, and all the birds beneath the sky came whirring and crowding in, and alighted around the ashes. And the doves nodded with their heads and began pick, pick, pick, pick, and the others began also pick, pick, pick, pick, and gathered all the good seeds into the dishes. And before half an hour was over, they had already finished and all flew out again.

Then Cinderella carried the dishes to the step-mother and was delighted, and believed that she might now go with them to the festival. But the step-mother said, "All this will not help you; you cannot go with us, for you have no clothes and cannot dance; we would be ashamed of you!" On this, she turned her back on Cinderella and hurried away with her two proud daughters.

As no one was now at home, Cinderella went to her mother's   grave beneath the hazel-tree and cried, "Shiver and quiver, little tree. Silver and gold throw down over me."

It was then that the bird threw a gold and silver dress down to her and slippers embroidered with silk and silver. She put on the dress as fast as she could and went to the festival. Her step-sisters and the step-mother, however, did not recognize her, and thought she must be a foreign princess, for she looked so beautiful in the golden dress. They never once thought of Cinderella and believed that she was sitting at home in the dirt, picking lentils out of the ashes.

The prince went to meet her, took her by the hand, and danced with her. He would dance with no other maiden, and never let go of her hand. If anyone else came to invite her, he said, "This is my partner."

She danced until it was evening and then she wanted to go home. But the King's son said, "I will go with you and keep you company," for he wished to see to where the beautiful maiden lived. She escaped from him, however, and sprang into the pigeon-house. The King's son waited until her father came, and then he told him that the beautiful young woman had leapt into the pigeon-house.

The old man thought, "Can it be Cinderella?" And they had to bring him an axe and a pickaxe that he could hack the pigeon-house to pieces, but no one was inside it. And when they got home, Cinderella lay in her dirty clothes among the ashes, and a dim little oil lamp was burning on the mantle-piece. For Cinderella had jumped quickly down from the back of the pigeon-house and had run to the little hazel tree, and there she had taken off her beautiful clothes and laid them on the grave, and the bird had taken them away again, and then she had placed herself in the kitchen among the ashes in her grey gown.

The Complete Grimm's Fairy Tales

The next day when the festival began again, and her parents and the stepsisters had gone once more, Cinderella went to the hazel-tree and said, "Shiver and quiver, my little tree. Silver and gold throw down over me."

Then the bird threw down a much more beautiful dress than on the day before. And when Cinderella appeared at the festival in this dress, everyone was astonished at her beauty. The King's son had waited until she came, and instantly took her by the hand and danced with no one but her. When others came and invited her, he said, "She is my partner."

When evening came and she wished to leave, the King's son followed her and wanted to see into which house she went. But she sprang away from him and into the garden behind the house. There stood a beautiful tall tree on which hung the most magnificent pears. She clambered so nimbly between the branches like a squirrel that the King's son did not know where she was gone.

He waited until her father came, and said to him, "The stranger-maiden has escaped from me, and I believe she has climbed up the pear-tree."

The father thought, "Can it be Cinderella?" And he had an axe brought and cut the tree down, but no one was on it. And when they got into the kitchen, Cinderella lay there among the ashes as usual. For she had jumped down on the other side of the tree, had taken the beautiful dress to the bird on the little hazel-tree, and put on her grey gown.

On the third day, when the parents and sisters had gone away, Cinderella went once more to her mother's grave and said to the little tree, "Shiver and quiver, my little tree. Silver and gold throw down over me."

And now the bird threw down to her a dress, which was even more splendid and magnificent than any she had yet had, and a pair of golden slippers. When she went to the festival in the dress, no one knew how to speak for astonishment. The King's son danced with her only, and if anyone invited her to dance, he said, "She is my partner."

When evening came, Cinderella wished to leave and the King's son was anxious to go with her, but she escaped from him so quickly that he could not follow her. The King's son had, however, created a strategy, and had caused the whole staircase to be smeared with pitch, and there, when she ran down, had the maiden's left slipper remained sticking.

The King's son picked it up, and it was small and dainty, and all golden. The next morning, he went with it to the father, and said to him, "No one will be my wife but she whose foot this golden slipper fits."

The two step-sisters were glad, for they had pretty feet. The eldest went with the shoe into her room and wanted to try it on, and her mother stood by. But she could not get her big toe into it because the shoe was much too small for her.

Then her mother gave her a knife and said, "Cut the toe off; when you are Queen you will have no more need for a foot."

The maiden cut the toe off, forced the foot into the shoe, swallowed the pain, and went out to the King's son. Then he took her on his his horse as his bride and rode away with her. They were, however, obliged to pass the grave, and there, on the hazel-tree, sat the two pigeons who cried, "Turn and peep, turn and peep. There's blood within the shoe. The shoe it is too small for her. The true bride waits for you."

The Complete Grimm's Fairy Tales

Then he looked at her foot and saw how the blood was streaming from it. He turned his horse around and took the false bride home again, and said she was not the true one, and that the other sister was to put the shoe on. Then this one went into her chamber and got her toes safely into the shoe, but her heel was too large. So her mother gave her a knife and said, "Cut a bit off your heel; when you are Queen you will have no more need for a foot."

The maiden cut a bit off her heel, forced her foot into the shoe, swallowed the pain, and went out to the King's son. He took her on his horse as his bride, and rode away with her, but when they passed by the hazel-tree, two little pigeons sat on it and cried, "Turn and peep, turn and peep. There's blood within the shoe. The shoe, it is too small for her. The true bride waits for you."

He looked down at her foot and saw how the blood was running out of her shoe, and how it had stained her white stocking. Then he turned his horse and took the false bride home again. "This also is not the right one," he said, "have you no other daughter?"

"No," said the man, "There is still a little stunted kitchen-wench which my late wife left behind, but she cannot possibly be the bride."

The King's son said he was to send her up to him; but the mother answered, "Oh, no, she is much too dirty, she cannot show herself!"

He absolutely insisted on it, and Cinderella had to be called. She first washed her hands and face, and then went and bowed down before the King's son, who gave her the golden shoe. Then she seated herself on a stool, drew her foot out of the heavy wooden shoe, and put it into the slipper, which fit like a glove. And when she rose up and the King's son looked at her face, he recognized the beautiful maiden who had danced with him and cried, "That is the true bride!"

The stepmother and the two sisters were terrified and became pale with rage. He, however, took Cinderella on his horse and rode away with her. As they passed by the hazel-tree, the two white doves cried, "Turn and peep, turn and peep. No blood is in the shoe. The shoe is not too small for her. The true bride rides with you."

And when they had cried that, the two came flying down and placed themselves on Cinderella's shoulders, one on the right, the other on the left, and remained sitting there.

When the wedding with the King's son had to be celebrated, the two step-sisters came and wanted to get into favor with Cinderella and share her good fortune. When the betrothed sisters went to church, the elder was at the right side and the younger at the left, and the pigeons pecked out one eye of each of them. Afterwards as they came back, the elder was at the left, and the younger at the right, and then the pigeons pecked out the other eye of each. And thus, for their wickedness and falsehood, they were punished with blindness as long as they lived.

Little Red Riding Hood

ONCE UPON A TIME, there was a dear little girl who was loved by everyone who looked at her, but most of all by her grandmother, and there was nothing that she would not have given to the child. Once she gave her a little cap of red velvet, which suited her so well that she would never wear anything else; so she was always called Little Red-Cap.

One day her mother said to her, "Come, Little Red-Cap, here is a piece of cake and a bottle of wine; take them to your grandmother, she is ill and weak and they will do her good. Set out before it gets hot, and when you are going, walk nicely and quietly and do not run off the path, or you may fall and break the bottle, and then your grandmother will get nothing. When you go into her room, don't forget to say, 'Good-morning,' and don't peep into every corner before you do it."

"I will take great care," said Little Red-Cap to her mother.

The grandmother lived out in the wood, a mile and half from the village, and just as Little Red-Cap entered the wood, a wolf met her. Red-Cap did not know what a wicked creature he was, and was not at all afraid of him.

"Good-day, Little Red-Cap," he said.

"Thank you kindly, wolf."

"Where are you headed so early, Little Red-Cap?"

"To my grandmother's."

"What have you got in your apron?"

"Cake and wine; yesterday was baking day, so poor sick grandmother is to have something good, to make her stronger."

"Where does your grandmother live, Little Red-Cap?"

"Just under a mile farther on in the wood. Her house stands under the three large oak-trees, the nut-trees are just below; you surely must know it," replied Little Red-Cap.

The wolf thought to himself, "What a tender young creature! What a nice plump mouthful—she will be better to eat than the old woman. I must act craftily, so as to catch both."

So he walked for a short time beside Little Red-Cap, and then he said, "See Little Red-Cap, how pretty the flowers are about here—why do you not look round? I believe, too, that you do not hear how sweetly the little birds are singing. You walk gravely along as if you were going to school, while everything else out here in the wood is merry."

Little Red-Cap raised her eyes, and when she saw the sunbeams dancing here and there through the trees, and pretty flowers growing everywhere, she thought, "Suppose I take grandmother a fresh bouquet of flowers; that would please her too. It is so early in the day that I will still get there in good time."

And so she ran from the path into the wood to look for flowers. And whenever she had picked one, she fancied that she saw a still prettier one farther on, and ran after it, and so got deeper and deeper into the wood.

Meanwhile the wolf ran straight to the grandmother's house and knocked at the door.

"Who is there?"

"Little Red-Cap," replied the wolf. "She is bringing cake and wine; open the door."

"Lift the latch," called out the grandmother, "I am too weak, and cannot get up."

The wolf lifted the latch, the door flew open, and without saying a word he went straight to the grandmother's bed and devoured her. Then he put on her clothes, dressed himself in her cap, laid himself in bed, and drew the curtains.

Little Red-Cap, however, had been running about picking flowers, and when she had gathered so many that she could carry no more, she remembered her grandmother, and set out on the way to her.

She was surprised to find the cottage-door standing open, and when she went into the room, she had such a strange feeling that she said to herself, "Oh dear! How uneasy I feel today when usually I am so happy being with grandmother."

She called out, "Good morning," but received no answer; so she went to the bed and drew back the curtains. There lay her grandmother with her cap pulled far over her face, and looking very strange.

"Oh! grandmother," she said, "what big ears you have!"

"The better to hear you with, my child," was the reply.

"But, grandmother, what big eyes you have!" she said.

"The better to see you with, my dear."

"But, grandmother, what large hands you have!"

"The better to hug you with."

"Oh! but, grandmother, what a terrible big mouth you have!"

"The better to eat you with!"

And scarcely had the wolf said this, than with one bound he was out of bed and swallowed up Red-Cap.

When the wolf had appeased his appetite, he lay down again in the bed, fell asleep, and began to snore very loud.

The huntsman was just passing the house and thought to himself, "How the old woman is snoring! I must just see if she wants anything."

So he went into the room, and when he came to the bed, he saw that the wolf was lying in it. "Do I find you here, you old sinner!" he said. "I have long sought you!"

Then just as he was going to fire at him, it occurred to him that the wolf might have devoured the grandmother, and that she might still be saved, so he did not fire, but took a pair of scissors, and began to cut open the stomach of the sleeping wolf. When he had made two snips, he saw the little Red-Cap shining. And then he made two snips more, and the little girl sprang out, crying, "Ah, how frightened I have been! How dark it was inside the wolf."

After that, the aged grandmother came out alive also, but scarcely able to breathe. Red-Cap, however, quickly fetched great stones with which they filled the wolf's body, and when he awoke, he wanted to run away, but the stones were so heavy that he fell down at once, and died.

Then all three were delighted. The huntsman drew off the wolf's skin and went home with it; the grandmother ate the cake and drank the wine that Red-Cap had brought, and revived, but Red-Cap thought to herself, "As long as I live, I will never by myself leave the path to run into the wood when my mother has forbidden me to do so."

◆◆◆◆◆◆◆

The Complete Grimm's Fairy Tales

It is also related that once when Red-Cap was again taking cakes to her grandmother, another wolf spoke to her, and tried to entice her from the path. Red-Cap, however, was on her guard, and went straight forward on her way, and told her grandmother that she had met the wolf, and that he had said "good-morning" to her, but with such a wicked look in his eyes, that if they had not been on the public road she was certain he would have eaten her up.

"Well," said the grandmother, "we will shut the door, so that he can't come in." Soon afterwards the wolf knocked, and cried, "Open the door, grandmother, I am little Red-Cap, and am fetching you some cakes." But they did not speak, or open the door, so the grey-beard walked two or three times around the house, and at last jumped on the roof, intending to wait until Red-Cap went home in the evening, and then to chase her and devour her in the darkness. But the grandmother saw what was in his thoughts.

In front of the house was a great stone trough, so she said to the child, "Take the pail, Red-Cap. I made some sausages yesterday, so carry the water in which I boiled them to the trough."

Red-Cap carried until the great trough was quite full. Then the smell of the sausages reached the wolf, and he sniffed and peeped down, and at last stretched out his neck so far that he could no longer keep his footing and began to slip, and slipped down from the roof straight into the great trough, and was drowned.

Red-Cap went joyously home, and never did anything to harm anyone.

The Singing Bone

IN A FAR AWAY LAND, there was once great concern over a wild boar that laid waste the farmer's fields, killed the cattle, and ripped up people's bodies with his tusks. The King promised a large reward to anyone who would free the land from this plague; but the beast was so big and strong that no one dared to go near the forest in which it lived. At last, the King gave notice that whoever should capture or kill the wild boar would have his only daughter as a wife.

Now there lived in the country two brothers: sons of a poor man who declared themselves willing to undertake the hazardous enterprise. The elder, who was crafty and shrewd, volunteered out of pride; the younger, who was innocent and simple, from a kind heart. The King said, "In order that you may be more sure of finding the beast, you must go into the forest from opposite sides."

So the elder went in on the west side, and the younger on the east. When the younger had gone a short way, a little man stepped up to him. He held in his hand a black spear and said, "I give you this spear because your heart is pure and good; with this you can boldly attack the wild boar, and it will do you no harm."

He thanked the little man, shouldered the spear, and went on fearlessly. Before long, he saw the beast, which rushed at him; but he held the spear towards it, and in its blind fury it ran so swiftly against it that its heart was sliced in two. Then he took the monster on his back and headed home with it to the King.

As he came out at the other side of the wood, there stood at the entrance a house where people were making merry with wine and dancing. His elder brother had gone in here, and, thinking that after all, the boar would not run away from him, was going to drink until he felt brave. But when he saw his young brother coming out of the wood laden with his booty, his envious, evil heart gave him no peace. He called out to him, "Come in, dear brother. Rest and refresh yourself with a cup of wine."

The youth, who suspected no evil, went in and told him about the good little man who had given him the spear with which he had slain the boar.

The elder brother kept him there until the evening, and then they went away together. When in the darkness they came to a bridge over a brook, the elder brother let the other go first. When he was half-way across, he gave him such a blow from behind that he fell down dead. He buried him beneath the bridge, took the boar, and carried it to the King, pretending that he had killed it; whereupon he obtained the King's daughter in marriage. When his younger brother did not come back he said, "The boar must have killed him," and everyone believed it.

But as nothing remains hidden from God, so this black deed also was to come to light.

Years afterwards, a shepherd was driving his herd across the bridge, and saw lying in the sand beneath, a snow-white little bone. He thought that it would make a good mouth-piece, so he clambered down, picked it up, and cut out of it a mouth-piece for his horn. But when he blew through it for the first time, to his great astonishment, the bone began to sing:

"Ah, friend, you blow upon my bone! Long have I lain beside the water. My brother slew me for the boar and took for his wife the King's young daughter."

"What a wonderful horn!" said the shepherd. "It sings by itself; I must take it to my lord the King."

And when he brought it to the King, the horn again began to sing its little song. The King understood it all, and required the ground below the bridge to be dug up, and then the whole skeleton of the murdered man came to light. The wicked brother could not deny the deed, and was sewn up in a sack and drowned. But the bones of the murdered man were laid to rest in a beautiful tomb in the churchyard.

The Complete Grimm's Fairy Tales

Mrs. Fox's Wedding

ONCE UPON A TIME, there was an old fox with nine tails who believed that his wife was not faithful to him, and wished to test her. He stretched himself out under a bench, did not move a limb, and behaved as if he were stone dead. Mrs. Fox went up to her room, shut herself in while her maid, Miss Cat, sat by the fire and did the cooking.

When it became known that the old fox was dead, wooers presented themselves. The maid heard someone knocking at the door. She went and opened it, and it was a young fox, who said, "What are you up to, Miss Cat? Did I catch you sleeping?"

She answered, "I am not sleeping, I am awake. Do you know what I am making? I am boiling warm beer with butter so nice. Would you like to have some?"

"No, thank you, miss," said the fox. "What is Mrs. Fox doing?"

The maid replied, "She sits all alone, with a cry and a moan, weeping her little eyes red, because old Mr. Fox is dead."

"Please tell her, miss, that a young fox is here who would like to woo her."

"Certainly, young sir."

The cat goes up the stairs trip, trap. The door she knocks at tap, tap, tap, "Mistress Fox, are you inside?"

"Oh yes, my little cat," she cried.

"A wooer he stands at the door out there."

"Tell me what he is like, my dear? Does he have nine tails as beautiful as those of the late Mr. Fox?"

"Oh, no," answered the cat, "he has only one."

"Then I will not have him." Miss Cat went downstairs and sent the wooer away. Soon afterwards there was another knock, and another fox was at the door who wished to woo Mrs. Fox. He had two tails, but he did not fare better than the first. After this still more came, each with one tail more than the other, but they were all turned away, until at last one came who had nine tails, like old Mr. Fox.

When the widow heard that, she said joyfully to the cat, "Now open the gates and doors all wide and carry old Mr. Fox outside."

But just as the wedding was going to be solemnized, old Mr. Fox stirred under the bench, beat the crowd with a club, and drove them and Mrs. Fox out of the house.

The Elves and the Shoemaker

6&

First story

ONCE UPON A TIME, a shoemaker, by no fault of his own, had become so poor that at last he had nothing left but leather for one pair of shoes. So in the evening, he cut out the shoes that he wished to begin to make the next morning. And as he had a good conscience, he lay down quietly in his bed, commended himself to God, and fell asleep. In the morning, after he had said his prayers, and was just going to sit down to work, the two shoes stood quite finished on his table. He was astounded and did not know what to think of it.

He took the shoes in his hands to observe them closer, and they were so neatly made that there was not one bad stitch in them, just as if they were intended as a masterpiece. Soon after, a buyer came in, and as the shoes pleased him so well, he paid more for them than was customary, and with the money the shoemaker was able to purchase leather for two pairs of shoes. He cut them out at night, and the next morning was about to set to work with fresh courage; but he had no need to do so. For, when he got up, they were already made, and buyers who were not wanting, gave him money enough to buy leather for four pairs of shoes.

The following morning, too, he found the four pairs made. And so it went on constantly: what he cut out in the evening was finished by the morning, so that he soon had his honest independence again and at last became a wealthy man.

One evening not long before Christmas, when the man had been cutting out shoes, he said to his wife before going to bed, "What would you think if we were to stay up tonight to see who it is that lends us this helping hand?"

The woman liked the idea and lit a candle, and then they hid themselves in a corner of the room behind some clothes that were hanging up there, and watched. When it was midnight, two pretty little naked men came, sat down by the shoemaker's table, took all the work which was cut out before them and began to stitch, and sew, and hammer so skillfully and so quickly with their little fingers that the shoemaker could not turn away his eyes for astonishment. They did not stop until all was done and finished on the table. Then, they ran quickly away.

The next morning the woman said, "The little men have made us rich, and we really must show that we are grateful for it. They run about so and have nothing on. They must be cold. I'll tell you what I'll do: I will make them little shirts, and coats, and vests, and trousers, and knit both of them a pair of stockings, and you can make them two little pairs of shoes."

The man said, "I will be very glad to do it."

So, one night, when everything was ready, they laid their presents all together on the table instead of the cut-out work, and then concealed themselves to see how the little men would behave. At midnight they came bounding in, and wanted to get to work at once, but when they did not find any leather cut out, but only the pretty little articles of clothing, they were at first astonished, and then they showed intense delight.

They dressed themselves with the greatest rapidity, putting the pretty clothes on, and singing, "Now we are boys so fine to see. Cobblers we don't need to be."

Then they danced and skipped and leapt over chairs and benches. At last, they danced out the doors. From that time forth they came no more, but as long as the shoemaker lived, all went well with him and all his efforts were rewarded.

Second story

THERE WAS ONCE a poor servant-girl, who was industrious and cleanly and swept the house every day, and emptied her sweepings on the great heap in front of the door. One morning, when she was just going back to her work, she found a letter on this heap. Because she could not read, she put her broom in the corner and took the letter to her master and mistress, and behold it was an invitation from the elves, who asked the girl to hold a child for them at its christening.

The girl did not know what to do, but at length, after much persuasion, and as they told her that it was not right to refuse an invitation of this kind, she consented. The three elves came and brought her to a hollow mountain where the little folks lived. Everything there was small, but more elegant and beautiful than can be described.

The baby's mother lay in a bed of black ebony ornamented with pearls, the coverlids were embroidered with gold, the cradle was of ivory, the bath of gold. The girl stood as godmother and then wanted to go home again, but the little elves urgently convinced her to stay three days with them.

So she stayed and passed the time in pleasure and gaiety, and the little folks did all they could to make her happy. At last, she set out on her way home. Before she could leave, they filled her pockets quite full of money, and after that they led her out of the mountain again.

When she got home, she wanted to begin her work and took the broom, which was still standing in the corner, in her hand and began to sweep. Then some strangers came out of the house and asked her who she was and what business she had there. And she had not, as she thought, been three days with the little men in the mountains, but seven years, and in the meantime, her former masters had died.

Third story
ONCE UPON A TIME, a mother's child had been taken away out of its cradle by the elves, and a changeling with a large head and staring eyes, which would do nothing but eat and drink, laid in its place. In her trouble, she went to her neighbor and asked her advice. The neighbor said that she was to carry the changeling into the kitchen, set it down on the hearth, light a fire, and boil some water in two eggshells, which would make the changeling laugh. If he laughed, all would be over with him.

The woman did everything that her neighbor told her. When she put the eggshells with water on the fire, the changeling said, "I am as old now as the Wester forest, but never yet have I seen anyone boil anything in an eggshell!" And he began to laugh at it.

While he was laughing, suddenly came a host of little elves, who brought the right child, set it down on the hearth, and took the changeling away with them.

The Godfather

☠

THERE WAS ONCE a poor man with so many children that he had already asked everyone in the world to be godfather. When yet another child was born, no one else was left whom he could invite. He knew not what to do, and in his perplexity, he lay down and fell asleep.

He dreamt that he was to go outside the gate and ask the first person who met him to be godfather. When he awoke, he was determined to obey his dream and went outside the gate and asked the first person who came up to him to be godfather. The stranger presented him with a little glass of water and said, "This is a wonderful water, with it you can heal the sick, only you must see where Death is standing. If he is standing by the patient's head, give the patient some of the water and he will be healed, but if Death is standing by his feet, all trouble will be in vain and the sick man will die."

From this time forth, the man could always say whether a patient could be saved or not. He became famous for his skill and earned a great deal of money. Once, he was called in to the child of the King. When he entered, he saw death standing by the child's head and cured it with the water. He did the same a second time, but the third time, Death was standing by its feet, and then he knew the child would die.

Later, the man decided to visit the godfather and tell him how he had succeeded with the water. But when he entered the house, it was such a strange establishment! On the first flight of stairs, the broom and shovel were arguing and knocking each other about violently. He asked them, "Where does the godfather live?"

The broom replied, "One flight of stairs higher up."

When he came to the second flight, he saw a heap of dead fingers. He asked, "Where does the godfather live?"

One of the fingers replied, "One flight of stairs higher."

On the third flight lay a heap of dead heads, which again directed him to the flight beyond. On the fourth flight, he saw fishes on the fire, which frizzled in the pans and baked themselves. They too said, "One flight of stairs higher."

When he had ascended the fifth, he came to the door of a room and peeped through the keyhole. There he saw the godfather who had a pair of long horns. When he opened the door and went in, the godfather got into bed in a great hurry and covered himself up. Then said the man, "Sir godfather, what a strange household you have! When I came to your first flight of stairs, the shovel and broom were quarreling, and beating each other violently."

"How stupid you are!" said the godfather. "That was the boy and the maid talking to each other."

"But on the second flight I saw dead fingers lying."

"Oh, how silly you are! Those were some roots of scorzonera."

"On the third flight lay a heap of dead men's heads."

"Foolish man, those were cabbages."

"On the fourth flight, I saw fish in a pan, which were hissing and baking themselves." When he said that, the fishes came and served themselves up.

"And when I got to the fifth flight, I peeped through the keyhole of the door, and there, godfather, I saw you and you had long, long horns."

"Oh, that is a lie!" The man became alarmed and ran out, and if he had not, who knows what the godfather would have done to him.

Fitcher's Bird

⌘

ONCE UPON A TIME, there was a wizard who used to take the form of a poor man and went to houses and begged and caught pretty girls. No one knew where he took them, for they were never seen again.

One day, he appeared before the door of a man who had three pretty daughters. He looked like a poor weak beggar and carried a basket on his back, as if he meant to collect charitable gifts in it. He begged for a little food, and when the eldest daughter came out and was handing him a piece of bread, he merely touched her, and she was forced to jump into his basket. At that moment, he hurried away with long strides, and carried her away into a dark forest to his house, which stood in the midst of it.

Everything in the house was magnificent. He gave her everything she could possibly desire, and said, "My darling, you will certainly be happy with me, for you have everything your heart could wish for."

This lasted a few days and then he said, "I must journey on and leave you alone for a short time. There are the keys of the house. You may go everywhere and look at everything except into one room, which this little key here opens, and if you go into that room I will punish you with death."

In addition to the keys, he gave her an egg and said, "Preserve the egg carefully for me, and carry it with you at all times, for a great misfortune would arise from the loss of it."

She took the keys and the egg, and promised to obey him. When he was gone, she went all around the house from the bottom to the top, and examined everything. The rooms shone with silver and gold, and she thought she had never seen such great splendor. At length she came to the forbidden door; she wished to pass it by, but curiosity let her have no rest.

She examined the key; it looked just like any other. She put it in the keyhole and turned it a little and the door sprang open. But what did she see when she went in? A great bloody basin stood in the middle of the room, and in it lay human beings, dead and hacked to pieces, and nearby was a block of wood and a gleaming axe lay upon it. She was so terribly alarmed that the egg, which she held in her hand, fell into the basin.

She got it out and washed the blood off, but somehow, it appeared again in a moment. She washed and scrubbed, but she could not get it out.

It was not long before the man came back from his journey, and the first things he asked for were the key and the egg. She gave them to him, but she trembled as she did so, and he saw at once by the red spots that she had been in the bloody chamber. "Since you have gone into the room against my will," he said, "you will go back into it against your own. Your life is ended."

He threw her down, dragged her by the hair, cut her head off on the block, and chopped her into pieces so that her blood ran on the ground. Then he threw her into the basin with the rest.

"Now I will fetch myself another," said the wizard, and again he went to the house in the shape of a poor man, and begged. When the second daughter brought him a piece of bread, he caught her like the first, by simply touching her, and carried her away.

She did not fare better than her sister. She allowed herself to be led away by her curiosity, opened the door of the bloody chamber, looked in, and had to atone for it with her life on the wizard's return. Then he went and brought the third sister, but she was clever and crafty. When he had given her the keys and the egg and had left her, she first put the egg away with great care, and then she examined the house, and at last went into the forbidden room.

Alas, what did she behold! Both her sisters lay there in the basin, cruelly murdered and cut into pieces. But she began to gather their limbs together and put them in order, head, body, arms, and legs. And when nothing further was left, the limbs began to move and unite themselves together, and both the maidens opened their eyes and were once more alive. Then they rejoiced and kissed and caressed each other.

On his arrival, the man at once demanded the keys and the egg, and as he could perceive no trace of any blood on it, he said, "You have stood the test, you will be my bride."

He no longer had any power over her, and was forced to do whatever she desired. "Oh, very well," she said, "you will first take a basketful of gold to my father and mother and carry it yourself on your back. In the meantime, I will prepare for the wedding."

Then she ran to her sisters, whom she had hidden in a little chamber, and said, "The moment has come when I can save you. The wretch will himself carry you home again, but as soon as you are at home send help to me."

She put both of them in a basket and covered them with gold, so that nothing of them was to be seen. Then she called in the wizard and said to him, "Now carry the basket away, but I will look through my little window and watch to see if your stop on the way to stand or to rest."

The wizard raised the basket on his back and went away with it, but it weighed him down so heavily that the perspiration streamed from his face. He sat down and wanted to rest awhile, but immediately one of the girls in the basket cried, "I am looking through my little window, and I see that you are resting. Please go on at once."

He thought it was his bride who was calling that to him and got up on his legs again. Once more, he was going to sit down, but instantly she cried, "I am looking through my little window, and I see that you are resting. Will you go on directly?"

Whenever he stood still, she cried this, and he was forced to go onwards until at last, groaning and out of breath, he took the basket with the gold and the two maidens into their parents' house.

Back at home, however, the bride prepared the marriage feast, and sent invitations to the friends of the wizard. She took a skull with grinning teeth, put some ornaments on it and a wreath of flowers, carried it upstairs to the garret window, and let it look out from there. When all was ready, she got into a barrel of honey, cut the feather-bed open, and rolled herself in it until she looked like a wondrous bird, and no one could recognize her.

Then she went out of the house and on her way, she met some of the wedding guests who asked, "O, Fitcher's bird, how did you get here?"

"I come from Fitcher's house quite near."

"And what may the young bride be doing?"

"From cellar to garret she's swept all clean. And now from the window she's peeping, I ween."

At last, she met the bridegroom, who was coming slowly back. He, like the others, asked, "O, Fitcher's bird, how did you get here?"

"I come from Fitcher's house quite near."

"And what may the young bride be doing?

"From cellar to garret she's swept all clean. And now from the window she's peeping, I ween."

The bridegroom looked up, saw the decked-out skull, thought it was his bride and nodded to her, greeting her kindly. But when he and his guests had all gone into the house, the brothers and kinsmen of the bride, who had been sent to rescue her, arrived. They locked all the doors of the house so that no one could escape, set fire to it, and the wizard and all his crew were burned.

The bride and her sisters lived happily ever after.

Old Sultan

A **FARMER ONCE** had a faithful dog called Sultan, who had grown old and lost all his teeth so that he could no longer hold anything in his mouth. One day the farmer was standing with his wife before the door, and said, "Tomorrow I intend to shoot Old Sultan, he is no longer of any use."

His wife, who felt pity for the faithful dog, answered, "He has served us so long and been so faithful, that we might well give him his keep."

"Eh! What?" said the man. "You are not very sharp. He has not a tooth left in his mouth, and not a thief is afraid of him; now he may be off. When he worked hard we fed him well; now his time is up."

The poor dog, who was lying stretched out in the sun not far off, had heard everything and was sad that tomorrow was to be his last day. He had a good friend, the wolf, and he crept out in the evening into the forest to him and complained of the fate that awaited him. "Don't worry about what you heard," said the wolf. "Be of good cheer, I will help you out of your trouble. I have thought of something. Tomorrow, early in the morning, your master is going with his wife to make hay, and they will take their little child with them, an no one will be left behind in the house. When they lay the child under the hedge in the shade for a nap, you lay yourself there too, just as if you wished to guard it. Then, I will come out of the wood, and carry off the child. You must rush swiftly after me, as if you would seize it again from me. I will let it fall and you will take it back to its parents, who will think that you have saved it, and will be far too grateful to do you any harm. On the contrary, you will be in high favor and they will never let you want for anything again."

The plan pleased the dog, and it was carried out just as it was arranged. The father screamed when he saw the wolf running across the field with his child, but when Old Sultan brought it back, then he was full of joy and stroked him and said, "Not a hair of yours will be hurt. You will eat my bread free as long as you live."

And to his wife he said, "Go home at once and make Old Sultan some bread soup that he will not have to bite, and bring the pillow out of my bed. I will give him that to lie upon."

Henceforth Old Sultan was as well off as he could wish to be.

Soon afterwards, the wolf visited him and was pleased that everything had succeeded so well. "To return the favor," he said, "I ask that you will just wink an eye if I have a chance to carry off one of your master's fat sheep."

"Do not reckon upon that," answered the dog. "I will remain true to my master; I cannot agree to that."

The wolf, who thought he deserved the favor, came creeping about in the night and was going to take away the sheep anyway. But the farmer, to whom the faithful Sultan had told the wolf's plan, caught him and whipped him soundly with a wooden stick. The wolf ran away, but he cried out to the dog, "Wait a bit, you scoundrel. You will pay for this."

The next morning, the wolf sent the boar to challenge the dog to come out into the forest so that they might settle the affair. Old Sultan could find no one to defend him but a cat with only three legs. As they went out together the poor cat limped along, and at the same time stretched out her tail into the air with pain.

The wolf and his friend were already at the spot they had decided on, but when they saw their enemy coming they thought that he was bringing a sabre with him, for they mistook the outstretched tail of the cat for one. When the poor cat hopped on its three legs, they could only think every time that it was picking up a stone to throw at them. They were both so afraid that the wild boar crept into the under-wood and the wolf jumped up in a tree.

When they arrived, the dog and the cat wondered why there was no one to be seen. The wild boar, however, had not been able to hide himself altogether and one of his ears was showing through the bushes.

While the cat was looking carefully around, the boar moved his ear. The cat, who thought it was a mouse moving there, jumped upon it and bit it hard. The boar made a fearful noise and ran away, crying out, "The guilty one is up in the tree."

The dog and cat looked up and saw the wolf, who was ashamed of having shown himself a coward. In the end, they made friends again and the Old Sultan was allowed to go on living with the farmer, and the wolf stayed away from the master's sheep.

The Complete Grimm's Fairy Tales

Sleeping Beauty

ONCE UPON A TIME, long, long ago, there were a King and Queen who said every day, "Ah, if only we had a child!" But they never had one. One day, when the Queen was bathing, a frog crept out of the water on to the land, and said to her, "Your wish will be fulfilled; before a year has gone by, you will have a daughter."

What the frog had said came true, and the Queen had a little girl who was so pretty that the King could not contain himself for joy and ordered a great feast. He invited not only his kindred, friends, and acquaintance, but also the wise women, in order that they might be kind and well-disposed towards the child. There were thirteen of them in his kingdom, but, as he had only twelve golden plates for them to eat out of, one of them had to be left at home.

The feast was held with all manner of splendor and when it came to an end the wise women bestowed their magic gifts upon the baby: one gave virtue, another beauty, a third riches, and so on with everything in the world that one can wish for.

When eleven of them had made their promises, suddenly the thirteenth came in. She wished to avenge herself for not having been invited, and without greeting or even looking at any one, she cried with a loud voice, "The King's daughter will in her fifteenth year prick herself with a spindle, and fall down dead."

And, without saying a word more, she turned around and left the room.

They were all shocked; but the twelfth, whose good wish still remained unspoken, came forward, and as she could not undo the evil sentence, but only soften it, she said, "It will not be death, but a deep sleep of a hundred years, into which the princess will fall."

The girl was cursed to become a sleeping beauty. The King, who would try to keep his dear child from the misfortune, gave orders that every spindle in the whole kingdom should be burned. Meanwhile the gifts of the wise women were plenteously fulfilled on the young girl, for she was so beautiful, modest, good-natured, and wise, that everyone who saw her was bound to love her.

It happened that on the very day when she was fifteen years old, the King and Queen were not at home, and she was left in the palace all alone. She went around into all sorts of places, looked into rooms and bed chambers just as she liked, and at last came to an old tower. She climbed up the narrow winding staircase, and reached a little door. A rusty key was in the lock, and when she turned it, the door sprang open, and there in a little room sat an old woman with a spindle, busily spinning her flax.

"Good day, old dame," said the King's daughter. "What are you doing there?"

"I am spinning," said the old woman, and nodded her head.

"What sort of thing is that, that rattles around so merrily?" said the girl, and she took the spindle and wanted to spin too. But scarcely had she touched the spindle when the magic decree was fulfilled, and she pricked her finger with it.

In the very moment when she felt the prick, she fell down upon the bed that stood there, and lay in a deep sleep. This sleep extended over the whole palace. The King and Queen who had just come home and had entered the great hall began to go to sleep, and the whole of the court with them.

The horses, too, went to sleep in the stable; the dogs in the yard; the pigeons upon the roof; the flies on the wall; even the fire that was flaming on the hearth became quiet and slept. The roast meat left off frizzling, and the cook, who was just going to pull the hair of the scullery boy because he had forgotten something, let him go and went to sleep. The wind stopped, and on the trees before the castle not a leaf moved again.

But around the castle there began to grow a hedge of thorns, which every year became higher, and at last grew close up around the castle and all over it, so that there was nothing of it to be seen, not even the flag upon the roof.

The story of sleeping beauty, for so the princess was named, travelled all over the country, so that from time to time kings' sons came to the area and tried to get through the thorny hedge into the castle. But they found it impossible. The thorns held tightly together as if they had hands. The youths would get caught in them, could not get loose again, and would die a miserable death.

After many long years, a King's son came again to that country and heard an old man talking about the thorn hedge, and that a castle was said to stand behind it in which a wonderfully beautiful princess, named Sleeping Beauty, had been asleep for a hundred years; and that the King and Queen and the whole court were asleep inside. He had heard, too, from his grandfather, that many kings' sons had already come and had tried to get through the thorny hedge, but they had remained stuck in it, and had died a pitiful death.

Still, the youth said, "I am not afraid. I will go and see the beautiful Sleeping Beauty."

The good old man tried to dissuade him, but the young man would not listen to his words.

By this time, the hundred years had just passed and the day had come when Sleeping Beauty was to awake again. When the King's son came near to the thorn hedge, it was nothing but large and beautiful flowers, which parted from each other of their own accord, and let him pass unharmed; then they closed again behind him like a hedge.

In the castle yard he saw the horses and the spotted hounds lying asleep. On the roof sat the pigeons with their heads under their wings. And when he entered the house, the flies were asleep upon the wall, the cook in the kitchen was still holding out his hand, and the maid was sitting by the black hen that she was going to pluck.

He went on farther, and in the great hall he saw the whole of the court lying asleep, and up by the throne lay the King and Queen.

He went on still farther, and all was so quiet that a breath could be heard, and at last he came to the tower and opened the door into the little room where Sleeping Beauty was sleeping. There she lay, so beautiful that he could not turn

The Complete Grimm's Fairy Tales

his eyes away. He stooped down and gave her a kiss. But as soon as he kissed her, she opened her eyes and awoke and looked at him quite sweetly.

Then they went downstairs together and the King awoke, and the Queen, and the whole court, and looked at each other in great astonishment. The horses in the courtyard stood up and shook themselves; the hounds jumped up and wagged their tails; the pigeons upon the roof pulled out their heads from under their wings, looked around, and flew into the open country. The flies on the wall crept again; the fire in the kitchen burned and flickered and cooked the meat; the joint began to turn and frizzle again, and the maid plucked the fowl ready for the spit.

The marriage of the King's son with Sleeping Beauty was celebrated with all splendor, and they lived happily ever after.

Snow White

ONCE UPON A TIME, in the middle of winter, when the flakes of snow were falling like feathers from the sky, a queen sat at a window sewing. While she was sewing and looking out of the window at the snow, she pricked her finger with the needle and three drops of blood fell upon the snow. The red looked pretty upon the white snow and she thought to herself, "I would love to have a child as white as snow, as red as blood, and as black as the wood of the window-frame."

Soon after that, she had a little daughter who was as white as snow, as red as blood, and her hair was as black as ebony. She called her Little Snow White. Soon after Little Snow White was born, the Queen died.

After a year had passed, the King married another wife. She was a beautiful woman but proud and haughty, and she could not bear that anyone else should surpass her in beauty. She had a wonderful mirror, and one day, she stood in front of it, looked at herself in it, and said, "Mirror, mirror, on the wall, who in this land is the fairest of all?"

The mirror answered, "You, O Queen, are the fairest of all!"

Then she was satisfied, for she knew that the mirror spoke the truth.

But Snow White was growing up, and grew more and more beautiful with each passing day. When she was seven years old she was as beautiful as the day, and even more beautiful than the Queen herself. One day, the Queen asked her mirror, "Mirror, mirror, on the wall, who in this land is the fairest of all?"

It answered, "You are fairer than all who are here, Lady Queen."
But more beautiful still is Snow White, as I ween."

The Queen was shocked. Her skin turned yellow and green with envy. From that hour, whenever she looked at Snow White, her heart heaved in her breast. She hated the girl so much.

Her envy and pride grew higher and higher in her heart like a weed, so that she had no peace day or night. She called a huntsman and said, "Take the child away into the forest. I will no longer have her in my sight. Kill her and bring me back her heart as a token."

The huntsman obeyed and took her away; but when he had drawn his knife and was about to pierce Snow White's innocent heart, she began to weep and said, "Ah dear huntsman, leave me my life! I will run away into the wild forest, and never come home again."

And because she was so beautiful, the huntsman had pity on her and said, "Run away, then, you poor child."

"The wild beasts will soon have devoured you," he thought, and yet it seemed as if a stone had been rolled from his heart because it was no longer necessary for him to kill her. And as a young boar just then came running by, he stabbed it, cut out its heart, and took it to the Queen as proof that the child was dead. The cook had to salt this, and the wicked Queen ate it, and thought she had eaten the heart of Snow White.

But now the poor child was all alone in the great forest and so terrified that she looked at every leaf of every tree and did not know what to do. Then she began to run. She ran over sharp stones and through thorns, and the wild beasts ran past her, but did her no harm.

She ran as long as her feet would go until it was almost evening; then she saw a little cottage and went into it to rest herself. Everything in the cottage was small, but neater and cleaner than can be told. There was a table covered with a white cloth and seven little plates. On each plate a little spoon; moreover, there were seven little knives and forks, and seven little mugs. Against the wall stood seven little beds side by side, and covered with snow-white comforters.

Little Snow White was so hungry and thirsty that she ate some vegetables and bread from each plate and drank a drop of wine out of each mug, for she did not wish to take all from one only. Then, because she was so tired, she laid herself down on one of the little beds, but none of them suited her. One was too long, another too short, but at last she found that the seventh one was right, and so she remained in it, said a prayer, and went to sleep.

When it was quite dark, the owners of the cottage came back. They were seven dwarfs who dug and mined in the mountains for ore. They lit their seven candles, and from the light within the cottage they saw that someone had been there, for everything was not in the same order in which they had left it.

The first said, "Who has been sitting on my chair?"

The second, "Who has been eating off my plate?"

The third, "Who has been taking some of my bread?"

The fourth, "Who has been eating my vegetables?"

The fifth, "Who has been using my fork?"

The sixth, "Who has been cutting with my knife?"

The seventh, "Who has been drinking out of my mug?"

The first dwarf looked around and saw that there was a little hole on his bed and he said, "Who has been getting into my bed?"

The others came up and each called out, "Somebody has been lying in my bed too."

But the seventh, when he looked at his bed, saw little Snow White who was lying there asleep. He called the others, who came running up, and they cried out with astonishment and brought their seven little candles and let the light fall on little Snow White.

"Oh, heavens! Oh, heavens!" they cried. "What a lovely child!" And they were so glad that they did not wake her up, but let her stay sleeping in the bed. The seventh dwarf slept with his companions, one hour with each, and so got through the night.

When it was morning little Snow White awoke and was frightened when she saw the seven dwarfs. But they were friendly and asked her what her name was.

"My name is Snow-white," she answered.

"How have you come to our house?" said the dwarfs.

Then she told them that her step-mother had wished to have her killed, but that the huntsman had spared her life and that she had run for the whole day, until at last she had found their dwelling.

The dwarfs said, "If you will take care of our house, cook, make the beds, wash, sew, and knit, and if you will keep everything neat and clean, you can stay with us and you will want for nothing."

"Yes," said Snow White, "with all my heart."

And she stayed with them. She kept the house in order for them. In the mornings they went to the mountains and looked for copper and gold. In the evenings they came back, and she would have their supper ready. The girl was alone the whole day, so the good dwarfs warned her, "Beware of your step-mother, she will soon know that you are here; be sure to let no one come in."

But the Queen, believing that she had eaten Snow White's heart, was sure that she was again the first and most beautiful of all. So, she went to her mirror and said, "Mirror, mirror, on the wall, who in this land is the fairest of all?"

The mirror answered, "Oh, Queen, you are the fairest of all I see. But over the hills, where the seven dwarfs dwell, Snow-white is still alive and well. And none is so fair as she."

The Queen was astounded, for she knew that the mirror never lied, and she knew that the huntsman had betrayed her, and that little Snow White was still alive.

So she thought and thought again how she might kill her, for as long as she was not the fairest in the whole land, envy let her have no rest. And when she had at last thought of something to do, she painted her face, and dressed herself like an old pedler-woman, and no one could have recognized her.

In her disguise, she went over the seven mountains to the seven dwarfs, and knocked at the door and cried, "Pretty things to sell, very cheap, very cheap."

Little Snow-white looked out of the window and called out, "Good-day my good woman, what have you to sell?"

"Good things, pretty things," she answered; "Laces of all colors," and she pulled out one which was woven of bright-colored silk.

"I may let the worthy old woman in," thought Snow White, and she unbolted the door and bought the pretty laces.

"Child," said the old woman, "what a fright you look; come, I will lace you properly for once."

Snow-white had no suspicion, but stood before her and let herself be laced with the new laces. But the old woman laced so quickly and so tightly that Snow White lost her breath and fell down as if dead.

"Now I am the most beautiful," said the Queen to herself, and ran away.

Not long afterwards, in the evening, the seven dwarfs came home, but how shocked they were when they saw their dear little Snow White lying on the ground, and that she neither stirred nor moved and seemed to be dead. They lifted her up, and when they saw that she was laced too tightly, they cut the laces. She began to breathe a little, and after a while came to life again. When the dwarfs heard what had happened they said, "The old pedler-woman was no one other than the wicked Queen; take care and let no one come in when we are not with you."

But the wicked woman when she had reached home went in front of her mirror and asked, "Mirror, mirror, on the wall, who in this land is the fairest of all?"

It answered as before, "Oh, Queen, you are the fairest of all I see. But over the hills, where the seven dwarfs dwell, Snow-white is still alive and well. And none is so fair as she."

When she heard that, all her blood rushed to her heart with fear, for she saw plainly that little Snow White was again alive.

"But now," she said, "I will think of something that will put an end to you."

By the help of witchcraft, which she understood, she made a poisonous comb. She then disguised herself and took the shape of another old woman. She went over the seven mountains to the seven dwarfs, knocked at the door, and cried, "Good things to sell, cheap, cheap!"

Little Snow White looked out and said, "Go away; I cannot let anyone come in."

"I suppose you can look," said the old woman, and pulled the poisonous comb out and held it up.

It pleased the girl so well that she let herself be beguiled, and opened the door. When they had made a bargain the old woman said, "Now I will comb you properly for once."

Poor little Snow-White had no suspicion and let the old woman do as she pleased, but hardly had she put the comb in her hair than the poison in it took effect and the girl fell down senseless.

"You paragon of beauty," said the wicked woman, "you are done for now," and she went away.

Fortunately, it was almost evening, when the seven dwarfs came home. When they saw Snow White lying as if dead upon the ground, they at once suspected the step-mother. When they looked around, they found the poisoned comb. Scarcely had they taken it out when Snow White came to life and told them what had happened. They warned her once again to be upon her guard and to open the door to no one.

The Queen, at home, went in front of the mirror and said, "Mirror, mirror, on the wall, who in this land is the fairest of all?"

It answered as before, "Oh, Queen, you are the fairest of all I see. But over the hills, where the seven dwarfs dwell, Snow-white is still alive and well. And none is so fair as she."

When the mirror spoke those words, she trembled and shook with rage. "Snow White will die," she cried, "even if it costs me my life!"

She went into a secret, lonely room, where no one ever came, and there she made a very poisonous apple. Outside it looked pretty, white with a red cheek, so that everyone who saw it longed for it; but whoever ate a piece of it would surely die.

When the apple was ready, she painted her face and dressed herself up as a country-woman, and so she went over the seven mountains to the seven dwarfs. She knocked at the door. Snow-white put her head out of the window and said, "I cannot let anyone in; the seven dwarfs have forbidden me."

"It is all the same to me," answered the woman, "I will soon get rid of my apples. There, I will give you one."

"No," said Snow-white, "I dare not take anything."

"Are you afraid of poison?" said the old woman; "look, I will cut the apple in two pieces; you eat the red cheek, and I will eat the white."

The apple was so cunningly made that only the red cheek was poisoned. Snow-white longed for the fine apple, and when she saw that the woman ate part of it she could resist no longer. She stretched out her hand and took the poisonous half. But hardly had she a bite of it in her mouth when she fell down dead.

The Queen looked at her with a dreadful look and laughed aloud and said, "White as snow, red as blood, black as ebony-wood! This time the dwarfs cannot wake you up again."

And when she asked of the mirror at home, "Mirror, mirror, on the wall, who in this land is the fairest of all?"

It answered at last, "Oh, Queen, in this land you are the fairest of all."

Then her envious heart had rest, so far as an envious heart can have rest.

The dwarfs, when they came home in the evening, found Snow White lying upon the ground; she breathed no longer and was dead. They lifted her up, looked to see whether they could find anything poisonous, unlaced her, combed her hair, washed her with water and wine, but it was all of no use. The poor child was dead and remained dead. They laid her upon a bier, and all seven of them sat around it and wept for her, and wept three days long.

They were going to bury her, but she still looked as if she were living and still had her pretty red cheeks.

They said, "We could not bury her in the dark ground."

Instead, they had a transparent coffin of glass made, so that she could be seen from all sides, and they laid her in it and wrote her name upon it in golden letters, and wrote that she was a king's daughter. Then they put the coffin out upon the mountain, and one of them always stayed by it and watched it. And birds came too and wept for Snow White; first an owl, then a raven, and last a dove.

And now Snow White lay a long, long time in the coffin. She did not change, but looked as if she were asleep; for she was as white as snow, as red as blood, and her hair was as black as ebony.

It happened, however, that a king's son came into the forest, and went to the dwarfs' house to spend the night. He saw the coffin on the mountain and the beautiful Snow White within it, and read what was written upon it in golden letters.

He said to the dwarfs, "Let me have the coffin, I will give you whatever you want for it."

But the dwarfs answered, "We will not part with it for all the gold in the world."

Then he said, "Let me have it as a gift, for I cannot live without seeing Snow White. I will honor and prize her as my dearest possession."

As he spoke in this way, the good dwarfs took pity upon him and gave him the coffin.

The King's son had it carried away by his servants on their shoulders. And it happened that they stumbled over a tree-stump, and with the bump, the poisonous piece of apple which Snow-white had bitten off came out of her throat. Before long, she opened her eyes, lifted up the lid of the coffin, sat up, and was once more alive.

"Oh, heavens, where am I?" she cried.

The King's son, full of joy, said, "You are with me," and told her what had happened, and said, "I love you more than everything in the world. Come with me to my father's palace and you will be my wife."

Snow-white was willing and went with him. Their wedding was held with great show and splendor, but Snow-white's wicked stepmother was also at the feast. She had arrayed herself in beautiful clothes and went before the mirror, and said, "Mirror, mirror, on the wall, who in this land is the fairest of all?"

The glass answered, "Oh, Queen, of all here the fairest art thou. But the young Queen is fairer by far as I trow."

The wicked woman uttered a curse, and was so wretched, so utterly wretched that she knew not what to do. At first, she would not go to the wedding at all, but she had no peace and had to go to see the young Queen. When she went in, she recognized the bride as Snow White. She stood still with rage and fear and could not move.

But iron slippers had already been put upon the fire, and they were brought in with tongs, and set before her. She was forced to put on the red-hot shoes and dance until she dropped down dead.

Thanks to the help of the seven dwarfs, and the accident with the coffin, Snow White and her husband lived happily ever after without ever worrying about that wicked witch again.

The Complete Grimm's Fairy Tales

Rumpelstiltskin

✂

ONCE UPON A TIME, there was a poor miller who had a beautiful daughter. One day, he had to go and speak to the King, and in order to make himself appear important he said to him, "I have a daughter who can spin straw into gold."

The King said to the miller, "That is an art which pleases me well. If your daughter is as clever as you say, bring her tomorrow to my palace, and I will watch what she can do."

When the girl was brought to him he took her into a room full of straw, gave her a spinning-wheel and a reel, and said, "Now set to work, and if by tomorrow morning early you have not spun this straw into gold during the night, you must die."

He locked up the room, and left her in it alone. So there sat the poor miller's daughter, and for the life of her could not tell what to do; she had no idea how straw could be spun into gold, and she grew more and more miserable, until at last she began to weep.

But all at once the door opened, and in came a little man who said, "Good evening, Mistress Miller. Why are you crying so?"

"Alas!" answered the girl, "I have to spin straw into gold, and I do not know how to do it."

"What will you give me," said the little man, "if I do it for you?"

"My necklace," said the girl.

The little man took the necklace, seated himself in front of the wheel, and whirr, whirr, whirr, three turns, and the reel was full; then he put another on, and whirr, whirr, whirr, three times around, and the second was full too. And so it went on until the morning when all the straw was spun and all the reels were full of gold.

By daybreak, the King was already there, and when he saw the gold, he was astonished and delighted, but his heart became only more greedy. He had the miller's daughter taken into another room full of straw which was much larger and commanded her to spin that also in one night if she valued her life.

The girl knew not how to help herself and was crying when the door again opened and the little man appeared and said, "What will you give me if I spin that straw into gold for you?"

"The ring on my finger," answered the girl.

The little man took the ring, again began to turn the wheel, and by morning had spun all the straw into glittering gold.

The King rejoiced beyond measure at the sight, but still he wanted more gold. He had the miller's daughter taken into a still larger room full of straw and said, "You must spin this, too, in the course of this night; but if you succeed, you will be my wife."

"Even if she be a miller's daughter," thought he, "I could not find a richer wife in the whole world."

When the girl was alone the little man came again for the third time, and said, "What will you give me if I spin the straw for you this time also?"

"I have nothing left that I could give," answered the girl.

"Then promise me, if you should become Queen, you will give me your first child."

"Who knows whether that will ever happen?" thought the miller's daughter; and, not knowing how else to help herself in this strait, she promised the small man what he wanted, and for that he once more span the straw into gold.

When the King came in the morning and found all as he had wished, he took her in marriage, and the pretty miller's daughter became a Queen.

A year after, she had a beautiful child, and she never gave a thought to the promise she made to the little man. But suddenly he came into her room and said, "Now give me what you promised."

The Queen was horror-struck and offered him all the riches of the kingdom if he would leave her the child.

But the little man said, "No, something that is living is dearer to me than all the treasures in the world."

Then the Queen began to weep and cry so that the little man pitied her. "I will give you three days' time," he said, "if by that time you find out my name, then you can keep your child."

So the Queen thought the whole night of all the names that she had ever heard, and she sent a messenger over the country to inquire, far and wide, for any other names that there might be. When the little man came the next day, she began with Caspar, Melchior, Balthazar, and said all the names she knew, one after another; but to everyone the little man said, "That is not my name."

On the second day she had inquiries made in the neighborhood as to the names of the people there, and she repeated to him the most uncommon and curious.

"Perhaps your name is Shortribs, or Sheepshanks, or Laceleg?"

But he always answered, "That is not my name."

On the third day, the messenger came back again and said, "I have not been able to find a single new name, but as I came to a high mountain at the end of the forest, where the fox and the hare bid each other good night, there I saw a little house, and before the house a fire was burning, and round about the fire quite a ridiculous little man was jumping: he hopped upon one leg, and shouted:

"Today I bake, tomorrow brew. The next I'll have the young Queen's child. Ha! glad am I that no one knew that Rumpelstiltskin I am styled."

You can imagine how glad the Queen was when she heard the name! And when, soon afterwards, the little man came in and asked, "Now, Mistress Queen, what is my name?"

At first she said, "Is your name Conrad?"

"No."

"Is your name Harry?"

"No."

"Perhaps your name is Rumpelstiltskin?"

"The devil has told you that! the devil has told you that!" cried the little man, and in his anger he plunged his right foot so deep into the earth that his whole leg went in. And then in a rage, he pulled at his left leg so hard with both hands that he tore himself in two.

The Queen was left to live in peace with her baby and the King, happily ever after.

The Three Feathers

♥

ONCE UPON A TIME, there was a King who had three sons, of whom two were clever and wise, but the third did not speak much. He was simple and so they called him the Simpleton.

When the King had become old and weak and was thinking of his end, he did not know which of his sons should inherit the kingdom after him. He said to them, "Go forth, and he who brings me the most beautiful carpet will be King after my death."

And so there would be no dispute among them, he took them outside his castle, blew three feathers in the air, and said, "You will go as they fly."

One feather flew to the east, the other to the west, but the third flew straight up and did not fly far, but soon fell to the ground. And now one brother went to the right, and the other to the left, and they mocked Simpleton, who was forced to stay where the third feather had fallen.

He sat down and was sad, when all at once, he saw that there was a trap-door close by the feather. He raised it up, found some steps, and went down them. At the bottom of the stairs, he came to another door, knocked at it, and heard somebody inside calling:

"Little green maiden small, hopping hither and thither;
Hop to the door, and quickly see who is there."

The door opened and he saw a great, fat toad sitting and
around her a crowd of little toads. The fat toad asked what
he wanted.

He answered, "I should like to have the prettiest and
finest carpet in the world."

The toad called a young one and said, "Little green
maiden   small,
hopping hither and thither. Hop quickly and bring me the
great box here."

The young toad brought the box and the fat toad opened
it, and gave Simpleton a carpet out of it. The carpet was so
beautiful and so fine that on the earth above, none could
have been woven like it. The Simpleton thanked her, and
ascended again.

The two others had, however, looked on their youngest
brother as so stupid that they believed he would find and
bring nothing at all. "Why should we give ourselves a great
deal of trouble to search?" they said, and got some coarse
handkerchiefs from the first shepherds' wives whom they
met, and carried them home to the King.

At the same time, Simpleton came back and brought his
beautiful carpet. When the King saw it, he was astonished
and said, "If justice be done, the kingdom belongs to the
youngest."

But the two others let their father have no peace, and said
that it was impossible that Simpleton, who in everything
lacked understanding, should be King, and entreated him to
make a new agreement with them.

The father then said, "He who brings me the most beautiful ring will inherit the kingdom."

He led the three brothers out and blew into the air three feathers, which they were to follow. Those of the two eldest again went east and west, and Simpleton's feather flew straight up and fell down near the door into the earth.

This time, he went down again to the fat toad and told her that he wanted the most beautiful ring. She at once ordered her great box to be brought and gave him a ring out of it, which sparkled with jewels, and was so beautiful that no goldsmith on earth would have been able to make it.

The two eldest sons laughed at Simpleton for going to seek a golden ring. They gave themselves no trouble, but knocked the nails out of an old carriage-ring, and took it to the King. But when Simpleton produced his golden ring, his father again said, "The kingdom belongs to him."

The two eldest did not cease from tormenting the King until he made a third condition and declared that the one who brought the most beautiful woman home should have the kingdom. He again blew the three feathers into the air, and they flew as before.

Simpleton, without further ado, went down to the fat toad and said, "I am to take home the most beautiful woman!"

"Oh," answered the toad, "the most beautiful woman! She is not at hand at the moment, but still you will have her."

She gave him a yellow turnip that had been hollowed out, to which six mice were harnessed.

Simpleton said quite mournfully, "What am I to do with that?"

The toad answered, "Just put one of my little toads into it."

He chose one at random out of the circle and put her into the yellow coach, but hardly was she seated inside it than she turned into a wonderfully beautiful maiden, and the turnip into a coach, and the six mice into horses. At this, he kissed her and drove off quickly with the horses and took her to the King.

His brothers came afterward; they had given themselves no trouble at all to seek beautiful girls, but had brought with them the first peasant women they met. When the King saw them he said, "After my death the kingdom belongs to my youngest son."

But the two eldest deafened the King's ears again with their clamor. "We cannot consent to Simpleton's being King."

They demanded that the one whose wife could leap through a ring which hung in the centre of the hall should have the preference. They thought, "The peasant women can do that easily; they are strong enough, but the delicate maiden will jump herself to death."

The aged King agreed likewise to this. The two peasant women jumped and jumped through the ring, but were so stout that they fell, and their coarse arms and legs broke in two. Then the pretty maiden, whom Simpleton had brought with him, sprang and sprang through as lightly as a deer, and all opposition had to cease.

He received the crown and has ruled wisely ever since.

Beauty and the Beast

ONCE UPON A TIME, there was a man who was about to set out on a long journey. Before he left, he asked his three daughters what he should bring back with him for them. His eldest daughter wished for pearls, the second wished for diamonds, but the third said, "Dear father, I should like a singing, soaring lark."

The father said, "Yes, if I can get it, you will have it," kissed all three, and set out.

Now when the time had come for him to be on his way home again, he had brought pearls and diamonds for the two eldest, but he had sought everywhere in vain for a singing, soaring lark for the youngest, and he was very unhappy about it, for she was his favorite child.

As he journeyed home, he went through a forest, and in the midst of it was a splendid castle, and near the castle stood a tree, and on the top of the tree, he saw a singing, soaring lark.

"Aha, you come just at the right moment!" he said, quite delighted, and called to his servant to climb up and catch the little creature. But as the servant approached the tree, a lion leapt from beneath it, shook himself, and roared till the leaves on the trees trembled.

"He who tries to steal my singing, soaring lark," he cried, "will I devour."

Then the man said, "I did not know that the bird belonged to you. I will make amends for the wrong I have done and ransom myself with a large sum of money if you will spare my life."

The lion said, "Nothing can save you unless you promise to give me what first meets you on your return home. If you will do that, I will let you live, and you will have the bird for your daughter in the bargain."

The man hesitated and said, "That might be my youngest daughter. She loves me best and always runs to meet me on my return home."

The servant, however, was terrified and said, "Why should your daughter be the very one to meet you, it might as easily be a cat, or dog?"

At that, the man allowed himself to be persuaded, took the singing, soaring lark, and promised to give the lion what ever should first meet him on his return home.

When he reached home and entered his house, the first who met him was no other than his youngest and dearest daughter, who came running up, kissed and embraced him, and when she saw that he had brought with him a singing, soaring lark, she was beside herself with joy.

The father, however, could not rejoice, but began to weep and said, "My dearest child, I have bought the little bird dear. In return for it, I have been obliged to promise you to a savage lion, and when he has you he will tear you in pieces and devour you," and he told her all, just as it had happened, and begged her not to go there, come what might.

She consoled him and said, "Dearest father, indeed your promise must be fulfilled. I will go and soften the lion so that I may return to you safely."

The next morning, she had the road pointed out to her, took leave, and went fearlessly out into the forest. The lion, however, was an enchanted prince and was by day a lion, and all his people were lions with him, but in the night they resumed their natural human shapes.

On her arrival, she was kindly received and led into the castle. When night came, the lion turned into a handsome man and their wedding was celebrated with great magnificence. They lived happily together, remained awake at night, and slept in the daytime.

One day he came and said, "Tomorrow there is a feast in your father's house, because your eldest sister is to be married, and if you are inclined to go there, my lions will escort you."

She said, "Yes, I should very much like to see my father again," and went to the wedding, accompanied by the lions.

There was great joy when she arrived, for they had all believed that she had been torn in pieces by the lion and had long ceased to live. She told them what a handsome husband she had and how well off she was, remained with them while the wedding feast lasted, and then went back again to the forest.

When the second daughter was about to be married, and she was again invited to the wedding, she said to the lion, "This time I will not be alone, you must come with me."

The lion, however, said that it was too dangerous for him, for if ray from a burning candle fell upon him, he would be changed into a dove, and for seven years long would have to fly about with the doves.

She said, "Ah, but do come with me. I will take great care of you, and guard you from all light."

So they went away together and took with them their little child as well. She had a chamber built so strong and thick that no ray could pierce through it. In this, he was to shut himself up when the candles were lit for the wedding feast. But the door of the chamber was made of green wood, which warped and left a little crack that no one noticed.

The wedding was celebrated with magnificence. When the procession, with all its candles and torches, came back from church and passed by the chamber, a ray as small as a hair fell on the King's son-in-law. When the ray touched him, he was transformed in an instant, and when she came in and looked for him, she did not see him, but instead saw a white dove sitting there.

The dove said to her, "For seven years must I fly about the world, but at every seventh step that you take, I will let fall a drop of red blood and a white feather. These will show you the way, and if you follow the trace you can release me."

After those words, the dove flew out the door and she followed him, and at every seventh step, a red drop of blood and a little white feather fell down and showed her the way.

She went further and further in the wide world, never looking about her or resting. When the seven years were almost past, she rejoiced and thought that they would soon be together. The truth is, they were so far from it!

Once, when they were moving onwards, no little feather and no drop of red blood fell, and when she raised her eyes the dove had disappeared. And as she thought to herself, "In this no man can help me," she climbed up to the sun, and said to him, "You shine into every crevice and over every peak, have you seen a white dove flying?"

"No," said the sun, "I have seen none, but I present you with a casket. Open it when you are in the greatest need."

She thanked the sun and went on until evening came and the moon appeared. She then asked the moon, "You shine the whole night through and on every field and forest, have you seen a white dove flying?"

"No," said the moon, "I have seen no dove, but here I give you an egg. Break it when you are in great need."

She thanked the moon and went on until the night wind came up and blew on her. Then she said to it, "You blow over every tree and under every leaf, have you seen a white dove flying?"

"No," said the night wind, "I have seen none, but I will ask the three other winds, perhaps they have seen it."

The east wind and the west wind came and had seen nothing, but the south wind said, "I have seen the white dove, it has flown to the Red Sea, where it has become a lion again, for the seven years are over and the lion is there fighting with a dragon. The dragon, however, is an enchanted princess."

The night wind then said to her, "I will advise you; go to the Red Sea. On the right bank are some tall reeds; count them, break off the eleventh, and strike the dragon with it. Then the lion will be able to subdue it, and both will regain their human form. After that, look around and you will see the griffin which is by the Red Sea. Swing yourself with your beloved, onto his back, and the bird will carry you over the sea to your own home. Here is a nut. When you are above the center of the sea, let the nut fall. It will immediately shoot up, and a tall nut-tree will grow out of the water on which the griffin may rest; for if he cannot rest, he will not be strong enough to carry you across, and if you forget to throw down the nut, you fall into the sea."

She went on and found everything as the night wind had said. She counted the reeds by the sea, and cut off the eleventh, struck the dragon with it, where upon the lion overcame it and immediately both of them regained their human shapes. But when the princess, who had before been the dragon, was delivered from enchantment, she took the youth by the arm, seated herself on the griffin, and carried him off with her.

There stood the poor maiden who had wandered so far and was again forsaken. She sat down and cried, but at last she took courage and said, "Still I will go as far as the wind blows and as long as the cock crows, until I find him."

And she went forth by long, long roads until at last she came to the castle where both of them were living together. There she heard that soon a feast was to be held, in which they would celebrate their wedding. She did not give up. Instead, she said, "God still helps me," and she opened the casket that the sun had given her.

A dress as brilliant as the sun itself lay inside. She took it out and put it on, and went up into the castle, and everyone, even the bride, looked at her with astonishment. The dress pleased the bride so well that she thought it might do for her wedding dress, and asked if it was for sale?

"Not for money or land," she answered, "but for flesh and blood."

The bride asked her what she meant by that, so she said, "Let me sleep a night in the chamber where the bridegroom sleeps."

The bride did not like the idea, yet she wanted very much to have the dress. At last she consented, but required the page to give the prince a sleeping potion.

When it was night, and the youth was already asleep, she was led into the chamber. She seated herself on the bed and said, "I have followed after you for seven years. I have been to the sun and the moon, and the four winds and have enquired for you, and have helped you against the dragon. How could you forget me?"

But the prince slept so soundly that it only seemed to him as if the wind were whistling outside in the fir trees. When the day broke, she was led out again and had to give up the golden dress. And as that had been of no avail, she was sad, went out into a meadow, sat down there, and wept. While she was sitting there, she thought of the egg that the moon had given her. She opened it, and out came a clucking hen with twelve chickens all of gold.

They ran about chirping, and crept again under the old hen's wings; nothing more beautiful was ever seen in the world! She rose and drove them through the meadow before her until the bride looked out of the window. The little chickens pleased the bride so much that she immediately came down and asked if they were for sale.

"Not for money or land, but for flesh and blood. Let me sleep another night in the chamber where the bridegroom sleeps."

The bride said, "Yes," intending to cheat her as on the former evening.

When the prince went to bed, he asked the page what the murmuring and rustling in the night had been. On this, the page told all: that he had been forced to give him a sleeping potion because a poor girl had slept secretly in the chamber, and that he was to give him another that night.

The prince said, "Pour out the potion by the bedside."

At night, she was again led in and when she began to relate how ill all had fared with her, he immediately recognized his beloved wife by her voice. He sprang to his feet and cried, "Now I really am released! I have been as it were in a dream, for the strange princess has bewitched me so that I have been compelled to forget you, but God has delivered me from the spell at the right time."

Then they both left the castle secretly in the night, for they feared the father of the princess, who was a sorcerer. They seated themselves on the griffin, which bore them across the Red Sea, and when they were in the midst of it, she let fall the nut. Immediately, a tall nut-tree grew up, where the bird was able to rest. The bird then carried them home, where they found their child, who had grown tall and beautiful, and they lived there happily ever after.

Hans My Hedgehog

ONCE UPON A TIME, there was a countryman who had lots of money and plenty of land, but though he was wealthy, he didn't feel happy because he had no children. Often, when he went into the town with the other peasants they mocked him and asked why he had no children. At last he became angry, and when he got home he said, "I will have a child, even if it be a hedgehog."

Soon after, his wife had a child, that was a hedgehog in the upper part of his body, and a boy in the lower, and when she saw the child, she was terrified, and said, "See, there you have brought bad luck on us."

The man said, "What can be done now? The boy must be christened, but we will not be able to get a godfather for him."

The woman said, "And we cannot call him anything else but Hans my Hedgehog."

When he was christened, the parson said, "He cannot go into any ordinary bed because of his spikes." So a little straw was put behind the stove, and Hans my Hedgehog was laid on it. His mother could not suckle him, for he would have pricked her with his quills. So he lay there behind the stove for eight years, and his father was tired of him and thought, "If he would but die!" He did not die, however, but remained lying there.

Now it happened that there was a fair in the town, and the peasant was about to go to it and asked his wife what he should bring back with him for her. "A little meat and a couple of white rolls which are wanted for the house," she said.

Then he asked the servant, and she wanted a pair of slippers and some stockings with clocks. At last he said also, "And what will you have, Hans my Hedgehog?"

"Dear father," he said, "do bring me bagpipes."

When the father came home again, he gave his wife what he had bought for her; meat and white rolls, and then he gave the maid the slippers and the stockings with clocks; and, lastly, he went behind the stove and gave Hans my Hedgehog the bagpipes. And when Hans my Hedgehog saw the bagpipes, he said, "Dear father, do go to the forge and get the cock shod, and then I will ride away, and never come back again."

On this, the father was delighted to think that he was going to get rid of him, and had the cock shod for him, and when it was done, Hans my Hedgehog got on it, and rode away, but took pigs and donkeys with him, which he intended to keep in the forest. When they got there he made the cock fly on to a high tree with him, and there he sat for many a long year, and watched his donkeys and pigs until the herd was quite large. All this time, his father knew nothing about him.

While he was sitting in the tree, he played his bagpipes, and made music that was very beautiful. Once a King came traveling by who had lost his way and heard the music. He was astonished at it, and sent his servant forth to look around and see from where this music came. He spied about, but saw nothing but a little animal sitting up aloft on the tree, which looked like a cock with a hedgehog on it making this music.

The King told the servant he was to ask why he sat there, and if he knew of the road that led to his kingdom. So Hans my Hedgehog descended from the tree and said he would show the way if the King would write a bond and promise him whatever he first came across in the royal courtyard when he arrived.

Then the King thought, "I can easily do that, Hans my Hedgehog understands nothing, and I can write what I like." So the King took pen and ink and wrote something, and when he had done it, Hans my Hedgehog showed him the way, and he got safely home. But his daughter, when she saw him from afar, was so overjoyed that she ran to meet him, and kissed him.

He quickly remembered Hans my Hedgehog and told her what had happened: that he had been forced to promise whatever first met him when he got home, to a very strange animal which sat on a cock as if it were a horse, and made beautiful music, but that instead of writing that he should have what he wanted, he had written that he should not have it. The princess was glad to hear this and said he had done well, for she never would have gone away with a Hedgehog.

Hans my Hedgehog, however, looked after his donkeys and pigs and was always merry and sat on the tree and played his bagpipes. Now it came to pass that another King came journeying by with his attendants and runners, and he also had lost his way and did not know how to get home again because the forest was so large.

He also heard the beautiful music from a distance and asked his runner what that could be and told him to go and find out. The runner went under the tree and saw the cock sitting at the top of it, and Hans-my-Hedgehog on the cock. The runner asked him what he was about up there.

"I am keeping my donkeys and my pigs; but what is your desire?"

The messenger said that they had lost their way and could not get back into their own kingdom. He asked if he would show them the way. Hans my Hedgehog came down the tree with the cock and told the aged King that he would show him the way on one condition: the King would give him whatever first met him in front of his royal palace.

The King said, "Yes," and wrote a promise to Hans my Hedgehog that he should have this. That done, Hans rode on before him on the cock and pointed out the way, and the King reached his kingdom again in safety. When he got to the courtyard, there were great rejoicings. Now he had only one daughter who happened to be very beautiful; she ran to meet him, threw her arms round his neck, and was delighted to have her father back again.

She asked him where in the world he had been so long. So he told her how he had lost his way and had very nearly not come back at all, but that as he was traveling through a great forest, a creature, half hedgehog, half man, who was sitting astride a cock in a high tree and making music, had shown him the way and helped him to get out, but that in return he had promised him whatever first met him in the royal court-yard, and how that was she herself, which made him unhappy now. But on this, she promised that for love of her father she would willingly go with this Hans if he came.

Hans my Hedgehog spent his time taking care of his pigs, and the pigs multiplied until they became so many in number that the whole forest was filled with them. That was when Hans my Hedgehog decided not to live in the forest any longer and sent word to his father to have every sty in the village emptied, for he was coming with such a great herd that there would be enough pigs for everyone. When his father heard the news, he was troubled, for he thought Hans my Hedgehog had died long ago.

Hans my Hedgehog seated himself on the cock, drove his pigs into the village, and ordered the slaughter to begin. The sounds of the slaughter were so loud, they could have been heard two miles off! Afterward, Hans my Hedgehog said, "Father, let me have the cock shod once more at the forge, and then I will ride away and never come back as long as I live." The father had the cock shod once more, and was pleased that Hans my Hedgehog would never return again.

Hans my Hedgehog rode away to the first kingdom. There the King had commanded that whoever came mounted on a cock and had bagpipes with him should be shot at, cut down, or stabbed by everyone, so that he could not enter the palace. So, when Hans my Hedgehog came riding into the kingdom, they all pressed forward against him with their pikes, but he spurred the cock and it flew up over the gate in front of the King's window and lighted there. Hans cried that the King must give him what he had promised, or he would take both his life and his daughter's.

The King began to speak his daughter fair, and to beg her to go away with Hans in order to save her own life and her father's. So she dressed herself in white, and her father gave her a carriage with six horses and magnificent attendants together with gold and possessions. She seated herself in the carriage and placed Hans my Hedgehog beside her with the cock and the bagpipes, and they took leave and drove away.

The King thought he would never see her again. He was, however, deceived in his expectation, for when they were at a short distance from the town, Hans my Hedgehog took her pretty clothes off and pierced her with his hedgehog's skin until she bled all over.

"That is the reward of your falseness," he said. "Go your way. I will not have you!" On that, he chased her home again, and she was disgraced for the rest of her life.

Hans my Hedgehog rode on further on the cock, with his bagpipes, to the dominions of the second King to whom he had shown the way. This one, however, had arranged that if any one resembling Hans my Hedgehog should come, they were to present arms, give him safe conduct, cry long life to him, and lead him to the royal palace.

But when the King's daughter saw him she was terrified, for he looked quite too strange. She remembered however, that she could not change her mind, for she had given her promise to her father. So Hans my Hedgehog was welcomed by her and married to her and had to go with her to the royal table. She seated herself by his side and they ate and drank.

When evening came and they wanted to go to sleep, she was afraid of his quills, but he told her she was not to fear, for no harm would befall her. He told the King that he was to appoint four men to watch by the door of the chamber and light a great fire, and when he entered the room and was about to get into bed, he would creep out of his hedgehog's skin and leave it lying there by the bedside. The men were to run nimbly to it, throw it in the fire, and stay by it until it was consumed.

When the clock struck eleven, he went into the chamber, stripped off the hedgehog's skin, and left it lying by the bed. Then came the men who fetched it swiftly and threw it in the fire. When the fire had consumed it, he was delivered! He lay there in bed in human form, but he was coal-black as if he, himself had been burned.

The King sent for his physician who washed him with precious salves and anointed him. He became white and was a handsome young man. When the King's daughter saw him, she was so happy. The next morning they arose joyfully, ate and drank, and then the marriage was properly solemnized, and Hans my Hedgehog received the kingdom from the aged King.

When several years had passed, Hans went with his wife to his father and confessed that he was his son. The father, however, declared he had no son he had never had but one, and he had been born like a hedgehog with spikes, and had gone forth into the world. Then Hans made himself known and the old father rejoiced and went with him to his kingdom where they all lived merrily together, happily ever after.

The Complete Grimm's Fairy Tales

The Blue Light

THERE WAS ONCE UPON a time a soldier who for many years had served the king faithfully, but when the war came to an end, he could serve no longer because of the many wounds which he had received. The king said to him: "You may return to your home, I need you no longer, and you will not receive any more money, for he only receives wages who renders me service for them."

The soldier did not know how to earn a living, went away greatly troubled, and walked the whole day, until in the evening he entered a forest. When darkness came on, he saw a light, which he went up to, and came to a house where there lived a witch. "Do give me one night's lodging, and a little to eat and drink," he said to her, "or I will starve."

"Oho!" she answered. "Who gives anything to a run-away soldier? Yet will I be compassionate, and take you in, if you will do what I wish."

"What do you wish?" said the soldier. "That you should dig all round my garden for me, tomorrow."

The soldier consented, and next day labored with all his strength, but could not finish it by the evening.

"I see well enough," said the witch, "that you can do no more today, but I will keep you yet another night, in payment for which you must tomorrow chop me a load of wood, and chop it small."

The soldier spent the whole day in doing it, and in the evening the witch proposed that he should stay one night more. "Tomorrow, you will only do me a very trifling piece of work. Behind my house, there is an old dry well, into which my light has fallen, it burns blue and never goes out, and you will bring it up again."

The next day the old woman took him to the well and lowered him down in a basket. He found the blue light and gave her a signal to draw him up again. She did draw him up, but when he came near the edge, she stretched down her hand and wanted to take the blue light away from him.

"No," he said, perceiving her evil intention. "I will not give you the light until I am standing with both feet upon the ground." The witch fell into a passion, let him fall again into the well, and went away.

The poor soldier fell without injury on the moist ground, and the blue light went on burning, but of what use was that to him? He saw very well that he could not escape death. He sat for a while very sorrowfully. Then suddenly he felt in his pocket and found his tobacco pipe, which was still half full. "This will be my last pleasure," he thought. He pulled it out, lit it at the blue light, and began to smoke.

When the smoke had circled about the cavern, a little black dwarf appeared before him, and said, "Lord, what are your commands?"

"What are my commands?" replied the soldier, quite astonished.

"I must do everything you bid me," said the little man.

"Good," said the soldier. "The first thing you can do is help me out of this well."

The little man took him by the hand, and led him through an underground passage, but he did not forget to take the blue light with him. On the way, the dwarf showed him the treasures which the witch had collected and hidden there, and the soldier took as much gold as he could carry. When he was above, he said to the little man, "Now go and bind the old witch, and take her before the judge."

In a short time she came by like the wind, riding on a wild tom-cat and screaming frightfully. Soon the little man reappeared. "It is all done," he said. "And the witch is already hanging on the gallows. What further commands do you have of me?"

"At this moment, none," answered the soldier. "You can return home, just promise to be at hand immediately, if I summon you."

"If you need to summon me, simply light your pipe at the blue light and I will appear before you at once." At that, the dwarf vanished from his sight.

The soldier returned to the town from which he come. He went to the best inn, ordered himself handsome clothes, and then asked the landlord to furnish him a room as handsome as possible. When it was ready and the soldier had taken possession of it, he summoned the little black dwarf and said, "I have served the king faithfully, but he has dismissed me and left me to hunger. Now I want to take my revenge."

"What do you need me to do?" asked the dwarf.

"Late at night, when the king's daughter is in bed, bring her here in her sleep. She will do servant's work for me."

The dwarf said, "That is an easy thing for me to do, but a very dangerous thing for you, for if it is discovered, you will pay a hefty price."

When twelve o'clock had struck, the door sprang open, and the dwarf carried in the princess. "Aha! Are you there?" cried the soldier. "Get to your work at once! Fetch the broom and sweep the chamber."

When she had done this, he ordered her to come to his chair, and then he stretched out his feet and said, "Pull off my boots." Then he threw them in her face and made her pick them up again and clean and brighten them. She, however, did everything he told her, without opposition, silently and with half-shut eyes.

Before morning came, the dwarf carried her back to the royal palace and laid her in her bed.

The next morning when the princess arose, she went to her father and told him that she had had a very strange dream. "I was carried through the streets at the speed of light," she said, "and taken into a soldier's room. I had to wait upon him like a servant, sweep his room, clean his boots, and do all kinds of menial work. It was only a dream and yet I am just as tired as if I really had done everything."

"The dream may have been true," said the king. "I will give you a piece of advice. Fill your pocket full of peas, and make a small hole in the pocket. If you are carried away again, they will fall out and leave a track in the streets."

But unseen by the king, the dwarf was standing beside him when he said that, and heard all. At night when the sleeping princess was again carried through the streets, some peas certainly did fall out of her pocket, but they made no track, for the crafty dwarf had just before scattered peas in every street there was. And again the princess was compelled to do servant's work until morning.

The next morning the king sent his people out to seek the track, but it was all in vain, for in every street poor children were sitting, picking up peas, and saying, "It must have rained peas, last night."

"We must think of something else," said the king. "Keep your shoes on when you go to bed, and before you come back from the place where you are taken, hide one of them there. I will soon contrive a way to find it."

The black dwarf heard this plot as well, and at night when the soldier again ordered him to bring the princess, revealed it to him. The dwarf told him that he knew of no good way to counteract the King's new strategy, and that if the shoe were found in the soldier's house it would be very bad for the soldier.

"Do what I say," replied the soldier. And again this third night the princess was obliged to work like a servant, but before she went away, she hid her shoe under the bed.

The next morning the king had the entire town searching for his daughter's shoe. It was soon found at the soldier's house. The soldier himself, who at the urgent request of the dwarf had gone outside the gate, was soon brought back and thrown into prison. In his fear, he had forgotten the most valuable things he had: the blue light and the gold. At present, he had only one coin in his pocket.

Now loaded with chains, he was standing at the window of his dungeon, when he happened to see one of his comrades passing by. The soldier tapped at the pane of glass, and when this man came up, he said to him, "Be so kind as to fetch me the small bundle I have left lying in the inn, and I will give you a ducat for doing it."

The comrade ran to the inn and brought back what he wanted. As soon as the soldier was alone again, he lit his pipe and summoned the black dwarf.

"Have no fear," said the dwarf to his master. "Go wherever they take you, and let them do what they will, only take the blue light with you."

The next day the soldier was tried, and though he did not deserve it, the judge sentenced him to death. When he was led forth to die, he begged one last favor of the king. "What is it?" asked the king.

"That I may smoke one more pipe on my way."

"You may smoke three," answered the king, "but do not think for a moment that I will spare your life."

The soldier pulled out his pipe and lit it at the blue light, and as soon as a few wreaths of smoke had ascended, the dwarf was there with a small club in his hand, and said, "What does my lord command?"

"Strike down to earth that false judge and his constable, and spare not the king who has treated me with such cruelty."

The dwarf fell on them like lightning, darting this way and that way, and whoever was so much as touched by his club fell to earth and did not venture to move again.

The king was terrified. He threw himself on the soldier's mercy and merely to be allowed to live at all, gave him his kingdom and his daughter to marry.

The Goose Girl

ONCE UPON A TIME, the king of a great land died and left his queen to take care of their only child. This child was a daughter who was very beautiful. Her mother loved her dearly and was very kind to her. There was a good fairy too, who was fond of the princess and helped her mother to watch over her.

When she grew up, she was engaged to be married to a prince who lived very far away. As the time drew near for her to be married, she got ready to set off on her journey to his country. The queen, her mother, packed up a great many costly things: jewels and gold and silver, trinkets, fine dresses, and in short everything that a royal bride would need. She gave her a servant to ride with her and give her into the bridegroom's hands; each had a horse for the journey. The princess's horse was the fairy's gift, and it was called Falada, and could speak.

When the time came for them to set out, the fairy went into her bedroom and took a little knife and cut off a lock of her hair. She gave it to the princess, and said, "Take care of it, dear child; for it is a charm that may be of use to you on your journey." Then they all said a sad goodbye to the princess. She put the lock of hair into her bosom, climbed on her horse, and set off on her journey to her groom's kingdom.

One day, as they were riding along by a brook, the princess began to feel very thirsty. She said to her maid, "Please get down and fetch me some water in my golden cup out of that brook, for I want to drink."

"No," said the maid. "If you are thirsty, get off yourself, and stoop down by the water and drink; I will not be your servant any longer."

She was so thirsty that she got down and knelt over the little brook and drank; for she was frightened and dared not bring out her golden cup. She wept and said, "Alas! What will become of me?"

The lock of hair she had been given answered her and said, "Alas! Alas! If your mother knew it, sadly, sadly, would she rue it."

But the princess was very gentle and meek, so she said nothing about her servant's bad behavior, and got on her horse again.

They rode farther on their journey until the day grew so warm and the sun so scorching that the bride began to feel very thirsty again. At last, when they came to a river, she had forgotten her maid's rude speech and said, "Please get down and fetch me some water to drink in my golden cup." But the maid answered her, and spoke even more haughtily than before.

"Drink if you will, but I will not be your servant"

The princess was so thirsty that she got off her horse and lay down. She held her head over the running stream and cried and said, "What will become of me?"

The lock of hair answered her again. "Alas! Alas! If your mother knew it, sadly, sadly, would she rue it."

And as she leaned down to drink, the lock of hair fell from her bosom, and floated away with the water. She was so frightened that she did not even see it; but her maid saw it and was very glad, for she knew the charm; and she knew that the poor bride would be in her power, now that she had lost the hair. When the bride was done drinking, and would have climbed on Falada again, the maid said, "I will ride on Falada and you may have my horse instead."

The princess was forced to give up her horse and soon afterwards, to take off her royal clothes and put on her maid's shabby ones.

At last, as they drew near the end of their journey, this treacherous servant threatened to kill her mistress if she ever told anyone what had happened. But Falada saw it all and remembered it well.

The servant got on Falada and the real bride rode upon the other horse. They went on in this way until at last they came to the royal court. There was great joy at their coming, and the prince flew to meet them. He lifted the servant from her horse, thinking she was the one who was to be his wife. She was led upstairs to the royal chamber, but the true princess was told to stay in the court below.

Now the old king happened just then to have nothing else to do; so he amused himself by sitting at his kitchen window, looking at what was going on. He saw her in the courtyard and noticed that she looked very pretty and too delicate to be a servant. He went up into the royal chamber to ask the bride who it was she had brought with her, who was left standing in the court below.

"I brought her with me for the sake of her company on the road," she said. "Please give the girl some work to do so that she will not be idle."

For some time, the old king could not think of any work for her to do, but at last he said, "I have a lad name Curdken who takes care of my geese; she may go and help him."

Later that day, the false bride said to the prince, "Dear husband, please do me one piece of kindness."

"That I will," said the prince.

"Tell one of your slaughterers to cut off the head of the horse I rode upon, for it was very unruly, and caused me nothing but trouble on our journey." The truth was, she was very much afraid that Falada would some day or other speak and tell everyone what she had done to the princess. She carried her point and the faithful Falada was killed.

When the true princess heard of it, she cried and begged the man to nail up Falada's head against a large dark gate of the city, through which she had to pass every morning and evening so that she might still see him sometimes. The slaughterer said he would do as she wished. He cut off the head and nailed it up under the dark gate.

Early the next morning, as she and Curdken went out through the gate, she said sorrowfully, "Falada, Falada, there you hang!"

The head answered, "Bride, bride, there you are! Alas! Alas! If your mother knew it, sadly, sadly, would she rue it."

Then they walked out of the city and drove the geese on. When she came to the meadow, she sat down upon a bank and let down her waving locks of hair, which were all of pure silver. When Curdken saw it glitter in the sun, he ran up, and would have pulled some of the locks out, but she

The Complete Grimm's Fairy Tales

cried, "Blow, breezes, blow! Let Curdken's hat go! Blow, breezes, blow! Let him after it go! Over hills, dales, and rocks, away be it whirled 'til the silvery locks are all combed and curled!"

Then there came a wind so strong that it blew off Curdken's hat; and away it flew over the hills. By this, he was forced to turn and run after it, and by the time he came back, she was done combing and curling her hair and had put it up again safe. This made him very angry and sulky, and he would not speak to her at all; but they watched the geese until it grew dark in the evening and then drove back home.

The next morning, as they were going through the dark gate, the poor girl looked up at Falada's head, and cried, "Falada, Falada, there you hang!"

The head answered: "Bride, bride, there you are! Alas! Alas! If your mother knew it, sadly, sadly, would she rue it."

Then she drove on the geese, sat down again in the meadow, and began to comb out her hair as before. Again, Curdken ran up to her and wanted to take hold of it, but she cried out quickly, "Blow, breezes, blow! Let Curdken's hat go! Blow, breezes, blow! Let him after it go! Over hills, dales, and rocks, away be it whirled 'til the silvery locks are all combed and curled!

Then the wind came and blew away his hat; and off it flew a great way, over the hills and far away, so that he had to run after it. When he came back she had bound up her hair again, and all was safe. So they watched the geese until it grew dark.

In the evening, after they came home, Curdken went to the old king and said, "I cannot have that strange girl helping me to keep the geese any longer."

"Why?" said the king.

"Because, instead of doing any good, she does nothing but tease me all day long."

It was then that the king made him tell him what had happened. Curdken said, "When we go in the morning through the dark gate with our flock of geese, she cries and talks with the head of a horse that hangs upon the wall, and says: 'Falada, Falada, there you hang!' And the head answers, 'Bride, bride, there you are! Alas! Alas! If they mother knew it, sadly, sadly, would she rue it.'"

Curdken went on telling the king what had happened in the meadow where the geese fed, how his hat was blown away and how he was forced to run after it and to leave his flock of geese to themselves. But the old king told the boy to go out again the next day. When morning came, he hid himself behind the dark gate and heard how she spoke to Falada and how Falada answered. Then he went into the field, and hid himself in a bush by the meadow's side; and he soon saw with his own eyes how they drove the flock of geese and how, after a little time, she let down her hair that glittered in the sun.

And then he heard her say, "Blow, breezes, blow! Let Curdken's hat go! Blow, breezes, blow! Let him after it go! Over hills, dales, and rocks, away be it whirled 'til the silvery locks are all combed and curled!

And soon came a gale of wind that carried away Curdken's hat, and away went Curdken after it, while the girl went on combing and curling her hair. All this the old king saw. So he went home without being seen, and when the little goose girl came back in the evening, he called her aside and asked her why she did so, but she burst into tears and said, "That I must not tell you or any man, or I will lose my life."

But the old king begged so hard, that she could not rest until she had told him the entire story, from beginning to end, word for word. And it was very lucky for her that she did so, for when she was done, the king ordered royal clothes to be put upon her and gazed on her with wonder. She was so beautiful. Then he called his son and told him that he had a false bride; for that she was merely a servant, while the true bride stood by.

The young king rejoiced when he saw her beauty and heard how meek and patient she had been. Without saying anything to the false bride, the king ordered a great feast to be prepared for all his court. The bridegroom sat at the top, with the false princess on one side and the true one on the other. Nobody recognized her, for her beauty was quite dazzling to their eyes, and she did not seem at all like the little goose girl now that she had her brilliant dress on.

When they had eaten and drank and were very merry, the old king said he would tell them a tale. So he began, and told all the story of the princess, as if it was one that he had once heard. He asked the false bride what she thought should be done to anyone who would behave in such a way.

"Nothing better," said this false bride, "than that she should be thrown into a cask stuck round with sharp nails, and that two white horses should be put to it and should drag it from street to street until she was dead."

"You are she!' said the old king. "And as you have judged yourself, that is what will be done to you."

The young king was then married to his true wife, and they reigned over the kingdom in peace and happiness all their lives; and the good fairy came to see them and restored the faithful Falada to life again.

Little Folk's Presents

ONCE UPON A TIME, a tailor and a goldsmith were traveling together. One evening, when the sun had sunk behind the mountains, they heard the sound of distant music, which became more and more distinct. It sounded strange, but so pleasant that they forgot all their weariness and stepped quickly onwards.

The moon had already risen when they reached a hill on which they saw a crowd of little men and women, who had taken each other's hands, and were whirling around in a dance with the greatest pleasure and delight. They sang most charmingly, and that was the music which the travelers had heard.

In the midst of them sat an old man who was rather taller than the rest. He wore a party colored coat, and his iron-gray beard hung down over his chest.

The goldsmith and the tailor remained standing full of astonishment and watched the dance. The old man waved for them to join, and the little folks willingly opened their circle. The goldsmith, who had a hump, and like all hunchbacks was brave enough, stepped in. The tailor felt a little afraid at first and held back, but when he saw how merrily all was going, he plucked up his courage, and followed.

The circle closed again directly, and the little folks went on singing and dancing with the wildest leaps. The old man, however, took a large knife that hung to his girdle, whetted it, and when it was sufficiently sharpened, he looked around at the strangers.

They were terrified, but they had not much time for reflection, for the old man seized the goldsmith and with the greatest speed, shaved the hair of his head clean off, and then did the same thing to the tailor.

Their fear left them when, after he had finished his work, the old man clapped them both on the shoulder in a friendly manner, as much as to say, they had behaved well to let all that be done to them willingly and without any struggle.

He then pointed with his finger to a heap of coals, which lay at one side, and signified to the travelers by his gestures that they were to fill their pockets with them. Both of them obeyed, although they did not know of what use the coals would be to them, and then they went on their way to seek a shelter for the night.

When they had arrived in the valley, the clock of the neighboring monastery struck twelve, and the singing ceased. In a moment all had vanished, and the hill lay in solitude in the moonlight. The two travelers found an inn and covered themselves up on their straw beds with their coats, but in their weariness forgot to take the coals out of them before doing so. A heavy weight on their limbs awakened them earlier than usual.

They felt in their pockets and could not believe their eyes when they saw that they were not filled with coals but with pure gold; happily, too, the hair on their heads and beards was there again as thick as ever. They had now become rich folks, but the goldsmith, who was quite greedy, had filled his pockets better and was twice as rich as the tailor.

A greedy man, even if he has much, still wishes to have more, so the goldsmith proposed to the tailor that they should wait another day and go out again in the evening in order to bring back still greater treasures from the old man on the hill.

The tailor refused and said, "I have enough and am content. Now I can be a master and marry my dear love (for so he called his sweetheart), and I am a happy man." But he stayed another day to please the goldsmith.

In the evening, the goldsmith hung a couple of bags over his shoulders so he could stow away a great deal of coal and took the road to the hill. He found, as on the night before, the little folks were singing and dancing. The old man again shaved his head clean and told to him to take some coal away with him.

He was not slow about sticking as much into his bags as would fit, and went back home quite delighted. He covered himself over with his coat. "Even if the gold does weigh heavily," he said, "I will gladly bear that," and at last he fell asleep with the sweet anticipation of waking up in the morning an enormously rich man.

When he opened his eyes, he got up in haste to examine his pockets, but how amazed he was when he drew nothing out of them but black coals. "Well, the gold I got the night before is still there before me," he thought, and went and brought it out, but how shocked he was when he saw that it also had turned back into coal!

He touched his forehead with his dusty black hand, and he could feel that his whole head was bald and smooth, as was the place where his beard should have been. But his misfortunes were not yet over; he now remarked for the first time that in addition to the hump on his back, a second, just as large, had grown in front of his chest. He quickly recognized the punishment of his greediness and began to weep out loud. The good tailor, who was awakened by this, comforted the unhappy fellow as well as he could, and said, "You have been my comrade in my traveling time; you will stay with me and share my wealth."

He kept his word, but the poor goldsmith was obliged to carry the two humps as long as he lived, and to cover his bald head with a cap.

The Complete Grimm's Fairy Tales

The Hare & the Hedgehog

⧗

THIS STORY, my dear young folks, sounds like it's false, but it really is true, for my grandfather, when relating it always used to say, "It must be true, my son, or else no one could tell it to you." The story is as follows.

One Sunday morning about harvest time, just as the buckwheat was in bloom, the sun was shining brightly in heaven, the east wind was blowing warmly over the stubble-fields, the larks were singing in the air, the bees buzzing among the buckwheat, the people were all going in their Sunday clothes to church, and all creatures were happy. The hedgehog was happy too.

The hedgehog, however, was standing by his door with his hands on his hips, enjoying the morning breezes, and slowly singing a little song to himself, which was neither better nor worse than the songs that hedgehogs are in the habit of singing on a blessed Sunday morning. While he was singing half aloud to himself, it suddenly occurred to him that while his wife was washing and drying the children, he might very well take a walk into the field, and see how his turnips were going on.

The turnips were, in fact, close beside his house, and he and his family were accustomed to eating them, for which reason he looked upon them as his own. No sooner said than done. The hedgehog shut the house-door behind him and took the path to the field. He had not gone very far from home and was just turning round the sloe-bush which stands there outside the field, to go up into the turnip-field, when he observed the hare, who had gone out to visit his cabbages.

When the hedgehog caught sight of the hare, he gave him a friendly good morning. But the hare, who was in his own way a distinguished gentleman and frightfully haughty, did not return the hedgehog's greeting, but said to him in a very contemptuous manner, "How do you happen to be running about here in the field so early in the morning?"

"I am taking a walk," said the hedgehog.

"A walk!" said the hare, with a smile. "It seems to me that you might use your legs for a better purpose."

This answer made the hedgehog furiously angry, for he could bear anything but an attack on his legs, because they were crooked by nature. So now the hedgehog said to the hare, "You seem to imagine that you can do more with your legs than I with mine."

"That is exactly what I think," said the hare.

"That can be put to the test," said the hedgehog. "I wager that if we run a race, I will outstrip you."

"That is ridiculous! You with your short legs!" said the hare. "But for my part I am willing, if you have such a monstrous fancy for it. What will we wager?"

"A golden coin and a bottle of brandy," said the hedgehog.

"Done," said the hare. "Shake hands on it and we'll race right now."

"No," said the hedgehog. "There is no such great hurry! I haven't eaten. I will go home first and have a little breakfast.

In half an hour I will be back again at this place." At that, the hedgehog departed, and the hare was quite satisfied.

On his way home, the hedgehog thought to himself, "The hare relies on his long legs, but I will contrive to get the better of him. He may be a great man, but he is a very silly fellow, and he will pay for what he has said."

So when the hedgehog reached home, he said to his wife, "Wife, dress yourself quickly, you must go out to the field with me."

"What is going on, then?" said his wife.

"I have made a wager with the hare for a gold coin and a bottle of brandy. I am to run a race with him, and you must be present."

"Good heavens, husband," the wife now cried, "are you out of your mind? Have you completely lost your wits? What can make you want to run a race with the hare?"

"Hold your tongue, woman," said the hedgehog, "that is my affair. Don't begin to discuss things which are matters for men. Go get dressed and come with me."

When they had set out on their way together, the hedgehog said to his wife, "Now pay attention to what I am going to say. I will make the long field our race-course. The hare will run in one section, and I in another, and we will begin the race from the top. All that you have to do is to place yourself here below in the furrow, and when the hare arrives at the end of the furrow on the other side of you, you must cry out to him, 'I am here already!'"

When they reached the field, the hedgehog showed his wife her place, and they walked up the field. When he reached the top, the hare was already there.

"Should we start?" said the hare.

"Certainly," said the hedgehog.

Each placed himself in his own furrow. The hare counted, "Once, twice, thrice, and away!" and went off like a whirlwind down the field. The hedgehog, however, only ran about three paces. Then he stooped down in the furrow and stayed quietly where he was.

When the hare arrived at the lower end of the field, the hedgehog's wife met him with the cry, "I am here already!" The hare was shocked and bewildered. He thought it was the hedgehog himself who was calling to him, for the hedgehog's wife looked just like her husband.

The hare, however, thought to himself, "That has not been done fairly," and cried, "It must be run again, let us have it again."

Once more he went off like the wind in a storm, so that he seemed to fly. But the hedgehog's wife stayed quietly in her place. So when the hare reached the top of the field, the hedgehog himself cried out to him, "I am here already."

The hare, quite beside himself with anger, cried, "It must be run again, we must have it again."

"All right," answered the hedgehog, "for my part we'll run as often as you choose."

So the hare ran seventy-three times more, and the hedgehog always held out against him, and every time the hare reached either the top or the bottom, either the hedgehog or his wife said, "I am here already."

At the seventy-fourth time, however, the hare was so tired, he could no longer reach the end. In the middle of the field he fell to the ground, the blood streamed out of his mouth, and he lay dead on the spot. The hedgehog took the gold coin which he had won and the bottle of brandy, called his wife out of the furrow, and both went home together in great delight, and to this day, they are living there still.

This is how it happened that the hedgehog made the hare run races with him until he died. And since that time, no hare has ever had any fancy for running races with a hedgehog.

The moral of this story is, firstly, that no one, however great he may be, should make fun of anyone else, even if he is only a hedgehog. And, secondly, when a man marries, he should chose a wife who looks just as he himself looks.

Tom Thumb

♈

ONCE UPON A TIME, a poor woodman sat in his cottage one
night, smoking his pipe by the fireside while his wife sat by
his side spinning. "How lonely it is, wife," he said, as he
puffed out a long curl of smoke, "for you and me to sit here
by ourselves, without any children to play about and amuse
us while other people seem so happy and merry with their
children!"

"What you say is very true," said the wife, sighing, and
turning round her wheel. "How happy I would be if I had
just one child! If it were ever so small, if it were no bigger
than my thumb-I should be very happy and love it dearly."

Now-odd as you may think it-it came to pass that this
good woman's wish was fulfilled, just in the very way she
had wished it; for, not long afterwards, she had a little boy
who was quite healthy and strong, but was not much bigger
than a thumb.

So they said, "Well, we cannot say we have not got what
we wished for, and, little as he is, we will love him dearly."
And they called him Thom Thumb.

They gave him plenty of food, yet for all they could do he
never grew bigger, but stayed the same size as he had been
when he was born. Still, his eyes were sharp and sparkling,

and he soon showed himself to be a clever little fellow who always knew well what he was about.

One day, as the woodman was getting ready to go into the woods to cut trees, he said, "I wish I had someone to bring the cart after me, for I want to work quickly"

"Oh, father," cried Tom, "I will take care of that; the cart will be in the wood by the time you want it."

The woodman laughed and said, "How can that be? You cannot reach up to the horse's bridle."

"Never mind that, father," said Tom. If my mother will only harness the horse, I will climb into his ear and tell him which way to go."

"Well," said the father, "we will try it just this once."

When the time came, the mother harnessed the horse to the cart and put Tom Thumb into the horse's ear. As he sat there, the thumb sized boy told the beast how to go, crying out, "Go on!" and "Stop!" as he wanted.

The horse went on just as well as if the woodman had driven it himself into the wood. It happened that as the horse was going a little too fast and Tom was calling out, "Gently! gently!" two strangers came up.

"What an odd thing that is!" said one. "There is a cart going along, and I hear a carter talking to the horse, but yet I can see no one."

"That is strange, indeed," said the other. "Let us follow the cart and see where it goes."

So they went on into the wood until they came to the place where the woodman was. Then Tom Thumb, seeing his father, cried out, "See father, here I am with the cart, safe and sound! Now take me down!" So his father took hold of the horse with one hand and with the other, took his son out of the horse's ear, and put him down upon a straw where he sat quite pleased and proud of himself.

The two strangers were all this time looking on and did not know what to think of this. At last, one took the other aside and said, "That little urchin will make us a fortune if we can get him and carry him about from town to town as a show. We must buy him." So they went up to the woodman, and asked him what he would take for the little man. "He will be better off," said they, "with us than with you."

"I won't sell him at all," said the father. "My own flesh and blood is dearer to me than all the silver and gold in the world."

But Tom, hearing of the bargain they wanted to make, crept up his father's coat to his shoulder and whispered in his ear, "Take the money, father, and let them have me; I'll soon come back to you."

So the woodman at last said he would sell Tom to the strangers for a large piece of gold, and they paid the price.

"Where would you like to sit?" said one of them.

"Oh, put me on the rim of your hat; that will be a nice gallery for me; I can walk about there and see the country as we go along." So they did as he wished; and when Tom had said goodbye to his father, they took him away with them.

They journeyed on until it began to be dusky, and then the little Tom Thumb said, "Let me get down, I'm tired." So the man took off his hat, and put him down on a clod of earth, in a plowed field by the side of the road. But Tom ran about among the furrows and at last slipped into an old mouse-hole.

"Good night, my masters!" he said. "I'm off! Mind and look sharp after me the next time."

The men ran at once to him and poked the ends of their sticks into the mouse hole, but all in vain; Tom only crawled farther and farther in. At last it became quite dark so that they were forced to go their way without their prize as sulky as could be.

When Tom was sure that they were gone, he came out of his hiding place. "What dangerous walking it is," he said, "in this ploughed field! If I were to fall from one of these great clods, I should undoubtedly break my neck." At last, by good luck, he found a large empty snail-shell. "This is lucky," he said, "I can sleep here very well," and in he crept.

Just as he was falling asleep, he heard two men passing by, chatting together. One said to the other, "How can we rob that rich clergymann's house and steal his silver and gold?"

"I'll tell you!" cried Tom.

"What noise was that?" said the thief, frightened. "I'm sure I heard someone speak."

They stood still listening, and Tom said, "Take me with you, and I'll soon show you how to get the clergyman's money."

"But where are you?" they asked.

"Look about on the ground," he answered, "and listen where the sound comes from."

At last the thieves discovered him and lifted him up in their hands. "You little urchin!" they said. "what can you do for us?"

"Why, I can get between the iron window-bars of the clergyman's house and throw you out whatever you want."

"That's a good thought," said the thieves. "Come along. We will see what you can do."

When they came to the clergyman's house, Tom slipped through the window bars into the room and then called out as loud as he could, "Will you have all that is here?" At this the thieves were frightened and said, "Softly, softly! Speak low, that you may not awaken anybody."

But Tom seemed as if he did not understand them, and bawled out again, "How much will you have? Should I throw it all out?" Now the cook lay in the next room; and hearing a noise she raised herself up in her bed and listened. In the meantime, the thieves were frightened and ran off a little way; but at last they plucked up their hearts and said, "The little urchin is only trying to make fools of us." So they came back and whispered softly to him, saying, "Now let us have no more of your roguish jokes; throw us out some of the money."

Then Tom called out as loud as he could, "Very well! Hold your hands! Here it comes."

The cook heard this quite plain, so she sprang out of bed and ran to open the door. The thieves ran off as if a wolf was at their tails, and the maid, having groped about and found nothing, went away for a light. By the time she came back, Tom had slipped off into the barn, and when she had looked about and searched every hole and corner, and found nobody, she went to bed, thinking she must have been dreaming with her eyes open.

Little Tom Thumb crawled about in the hay loft, and at last found a snug place to finish his night's rest. He laid himself down, meaning to sleep until daylight and then find his way home to his father and mother. But alas! How woefully he was undone! What crosses and sorrows happen to us all in this world!

The cook got up early, before daybreak, to feed the cows. Heading straight to the hay loft where Tom was sleeping, she carried away a large bundle of hay with Tom in the middle of it, fast asleep. He continued sleeping and did not awake until he found himself in the mouth of the cow; for the cook had put the hay into the cow's dish, and the cow had taken Tom up in a mouthful of it.

"What has gone wrong?" he thought. "Where on earth am I?" But he soon found out where he really was; and was forced to have all his wits about him so that he would not end up between the cow's teeth and be crushed to death. At last, down he went into her stomach.

"It is rather dark," he said. "They forgot to build windows in this room to let the sun in; a candle would helpful."

Though he made the best of his bad luck, he did not like his living quarters at all; and the worst of it was, that more and more hay was always coming down, and the space left for him became smaller and smaller. At last he cried out as loud as he could, "Don't bring me any more hay! Don't bring me any more hay!"

The maid happened to be just then milking the cow and hearing someone speak, but seeing nobody and yet being quite sure it was the same voice she heard the night before. She was so frightened that she fell off her stool and spilled the milk pail. As soon as she could pick herself up out of the dirt, she ran off as fast as she could to her master the clergyman, and said, "Sir, sir, the cow is talking!"

But the clergyman said, "Woman, you are surely crazy!" However, he went with her into the cow house to try and see what was the matter.

Scarcely had they set foot on the threshold, when Tom called out, "Don't bring me any more hay!" Then the parson himself was frightened; and thinking the cow was surely bewitched, told his servant to kill her on the spot. So the cow was killed and cut up; and the stomach in which Tom lay was thrown into a dunghill.

Tom soon set himself to work to get out of the cows stomach. It was not a very easy task but at last, just as he had made room to get his head out, more bad luck arrived. A hungry wolf sprang out, and swallowed up the whole stomach, with Tom in it, at one gulp, and ran away.

Tom, however, would not give up; and thinking the wolf might like having someone to chat with him as he was going along, he called out, "My good friend, I can show you a famous treat."

"Where's that?" said the wolf.

"In such and such a house," said Tom, describing his own father's house. "You can crawl through the drain into the kitchen and then into the pantry, and there you will find cakes, ham, beef, cold chicken, roast pig, apple-dumplings, and everything that your heart can wish."

The wolf did not want to be asked twice, so that very night he went to the house and crawled through the drain into the kitchen and then into the pantry, and ate and drank there to his heart's content. As soon as he had had enough, he wanted to get away, but he had eaten so much that he was too big to go out by the same way he came in.

This was just what Tom had hoped for. Now he began to create a great shout, making all the noise he could.

"Will you be easy" said the wolf. "You'll awaken everybody in the house if you make such a clatter."

"That doesn't matter to me," said little Tom. "You have had your frolic, now I've a mind to be merry myself," and he began singing and shouting as loud as he could.

The woodman and his wife, being awakened by the noise, peeped through a crack in the door; but when they saw a wolf was there, you may well suppose that they were very frightened. The woodman ran for his axe, and gave his wife a knife.

"You stay behind," said the woodman, "and when I have knocked him on the head you must rip him up with the knife."

Tom heard all this, and cried out, "Father, father! I am here. The wolf has swallowed me."

And his father said, "Heaven be praised! We have found our dear child again." At that, he told his wife not to use the knife for fear she could hurt him. Then he aimed a great blow and struck the wolf on the head and killed him on the spot! When he was dead, they cut open his body and set little Tom free.

"Ah!" said the father. "What fears we have had for you!"

"Yes, father," he answered, "I have traveled all over the world, I think, in one way or other, since we parted. And now I am very glad to come home and get fresh air again."

"Why, where have you been?" asked his father.

"I have been in a mouse hole and in a snail shell and down a cow's throat and in the wolf's belly; and yet here I am again, safe and sound."

"Well," they said, "you have come back and we will not sell you again for all the riches in the world."

Then they hugged and kissed their dear little son and gave him plenty to eat and drink, for he was very hungry.

Then they fetched new clothes for him, for his old ones had been quite spoiled on his journey. So Master Thumb stayed at home with his father and mother in peace; for though he had been so great a traveler and had done and seen so many fine things and was fond enough of telling the whole story, he always agreed that, after all, there's no place like home!

The Golden Goose

ONCE UPON A TIME, there was a man who had three sons. The youngest of his sons was called Dummling, and he was despised, mocked, and sneered at every occasion.

One day, the oldest son wanted to go into the forest to cut wood, and before he went, his mother gave him a beautiful sweet cake and a bottle of wine so that he would not suffer from hunger or thirst.

When he entered the forest, he met a little grey-haired old man who bade him good day, and said, "Do give me a piece of cake out of your pocket, and let me have a sip of your wine; I am so hungry and thirsty."

But the clever son answered, "If I give you my cake and wine, I will have none for myself. Go away." And he left the little man standing and went on.

But when he began to chop down a tree, it was not long before he made a missed stroke, and the axe cut him in the arm so that he had to go home and have it bound up. And this was the little grey man's doing.

After this, the second son went into the forest, and his mother gave him, like the eldest, a cake and a bottle of wine. The little old grey man met him and asked him for a piece of cake and a drink of wine. But the second son, too, said sensibly enough, "What I give you will be taken away from myself. Be off!" And he left the little man standing and went on.

His punishment, however, was not delayed. When he had made a few blows at the tree he struck himself in the leg, so that he had to be carried home.

Then Dummling said, "Father, do let me go and cut wood."

The father answered, "Your brothers have hurt themselves with it, leave it alone, you do not understand anything about it."

But Dummling begged for so long that at last his father said, "Just go then, you will learn your lesson the hard way when you hurt yourself."

His mother gave him a cake made with water and baked in the cinders, and with it a bottle of sour beer.

When he came to the forest the little old grey man met him likewise, and greeting him, said, "Give me a piece of your cake and a drink out of your bottle; I am so hungry and thirsty."

Dummling answered, "I have only cinder-cake and sour beer; if that pleases you, we will sit down and eat."

So they sat down, and when Dummling pulled out his cinder-cake, it was a fine sweet cake and the sour beer had become good wine. So they ate and drank, and after that the little man said, "Since you have a good heart and are willing to share what you have, I will give you good luck. There stands an old tree. Cut it down and you will find something at the roots." Then the little man disappeared.

Dummling went and cut down the tree. When it fell, there was a goose sitting in the roots with feathers of pure gold. He lifted her up, and taking her with him, went to an inn where he thought he would stay the night. Now the host had three daughters, who saw the goose and were curious to know what such a wonderful bird might be, and would have liked to have one of its golden feathers.

The oldest sister thought, "I will soon find an opportunity of pulling out a feather." And as soon as Dummling had gone out, she seized the goose by the wing, but her finger and hand became stuck to it.

The second sister came soon afterwards, thinking only of how she might get a feather for herself, but she had scarcely touched her sister when she found herself stuck there, as well.

At last, the third came with the same intent, and the others screamed out, "Keep away. For goodness sake keep away!" But she did not understand why she was to keep away. "The others are there," she thought. "I may as well be there too." She ran to them, but as soon as she had touched her sister, she became stuck to her. So all three of them had to spend the night with the goose.

The next morning, Dummling took the goose under his arm and set out, without troubling himself about the three girls who were hanging on to it. They were obliged to run after him continually, now left, now right, wherever his legs took him.

In the middle of the fields, the clergyman met them, and when he saw the procession he said, "Shame on you, you good-for-nothing girls, why are you running across the fields after this young man?" At the same time, he seized the youngest by the hand in order to pull her away, but as soon as he touched her, he became stuck as well and was obliged to run behind with the rest of them.

Before long, the church caretaker came by and saw his master, the clergyman, running behind three girls. He was astonished at this and called out, "Hi! Your reverence, where are you going so quickly? Do not forget that we have a christening today!" And running after him, he took him by the sleeve, but also become stuck to it.

While the five were running around, one behind the other, two laborers came with their hoes from the fields. The clergyman called out to them and begged for them to set him and the caretaker free. But they had scarcely touched the sexton when they became stuck. Now there were seven of them running behind Dummling and the goose.

Soon afterwards, the group came to a city where a king ruled who had a daughter who was so serious that no one could make her laugh. So he had put forth a reward that whoever was able to make her laugh could marry her. When Dummling heard this, he went with his goose, and all of the people stuck to him, before the king's daughter. As soon as she saw the seven people running on and on, one behind the other, she began to laugh quite loudly as if she would never stop.

At that moment, Dummling asked if she would be his wife; but the king did not like the son-in- law and made a bunch of excuses and said he must first produce a man who could drink an entire cellar of wine. Dummling thought of the little grey man, who could certainly help him; so he went into the forest, and in the same place where he had chopped the tree, he saw a man sitting, who had a very sorrowful face. Dummling asked him why he was so sad. The man answered, "I have such a great thirst and cannot quench it. Cold water I cannot stand, a barrel of wine I have just emptied, but that to me is like a drop on a hot stone!"

"There, I can help you," said Dummling. "Just come with me and I promise you will be satisfied."

He led the man into the king's cellar, and the man bent over the huge barrels, and drank and drank until he couldn't drink anymore. Before the day was out he had emptied all the barrels. Then Dummling asked once more for his bride, but the king was distressed that such an ugly fellow, whom everyone called Dummling, should take away his daughter, so he made a new condition: The man to marry his daughter must first find a man who could eat a whole mountain of bread.

Dummling did not think long, but went straight into the forest, where in the same place there sat a man who was tying up his body with a strap and making an awful face and saying, "I have eaten a whole ovenful of rolls, but what good is that when one has such a hunger as I? My stomach remains empty, and I must tie myself up if I am not to die of hunger."

At this Dummling was glad, and said, "Get up and come with me; you will eat yourself full." He led him to the king's palace where all the flour in the whole Kingdom was collected, and from it he ordered a huge mountain of bread to be baked. The man from the forest stood before it, began to eat, and by the end of one day, the whole mountain of bread had vanished.

Dummling, for the third time, asked for his bride; but the king again sought a way out and ordered a ship which could sail on land and on water. "As soon as you come sailing back in it,' he said, "you shall have my daughter for wife."

Dummling went straight into the forest, and there sat the little grey man to whom he had given his cake. When he heard what Dummling wanted, he said: 'Since you have given me to food eat and wine to drink, I will give you the ship; and I will do all of this because you once were kind to me." The man gave him the ship, which could sail on land and water, and when the king saw that, he knew he could no longer prevent Dummling from having his daughter.

The wedding was celebrated, and after the king's death, Dummling inherited his kingdom and lived with his wife, happily ever after.

The Crystal Ball

O

ONCE UPON A TIME, there was an enchantress who had three sons who loved each other as brothers, but the old woman did not trust them and thought they wanted to steal her power from her. So she changed the eldest into an eagle, which was forced to live in the rocky mountains, and was often seen flying in great circles in the sky.

The second, she changed into a whale, which lived in the deep sea, and all that was seen of it was that it sometimes spouted up a great jet of water into the air. Each of them bore his human form for only two hours a day.

The third son, who was afraid she might change him into a raging wild beast—a bear perhaps, or a wolf, went secretly away. He had heard that a king's daughter who was bewitched, was imprisoned in the castle of the golden sun and was waiting to be set free.

Those, however, who tried to free her risked their lives. Twenty-three youths had already died a miserable death, and now only one other would be allowed make the attempt, after which no more could come. And as his heart was without fear, he made up his mind to seek out the castle of the golden sun.

He had already traveled around for a long time without being able to find it, when he came by chance into a great forest and did not know the way out of it. All at once, he saw in the distance two giants, who made a sign to him with their hands. When he came to them they said, "We are quarreling about a cap, and which of us it is to belong to. And as we are equally strong, neither of us can get the better of the other. The small men are more clever than we are, so we will leave the decision to you."

"How can you dispute about an old cap?" said the youth.

"You do not know what properties it has. It is a wishing-cap. Whoever puts it on, can wish himself away wherever he likes, and in an instant he will be there."

"Give me the cap," said the youth, "and I will go a short distance off. When I call you, you must run a race and the cap shall belong to the one who reaches me first."

He put it on and went away, and thought of the king's daughter, forgot about the giants, and walked continually onward. At length he sighed from the very bottom of his heart and cried, "Ah, if I were but at the castle of the golden sun."

Hardly had the words passed his lips than he was standing on a high mountain before the gate of the castle. He entered and went through all the rooms, until in the last room he found the king's daughter. But how shocked he was when he saw her. She had an ashen-gray face full of wrinkles, bleary eyes, and red hair.

"Are you the king's daughter, whose beauty the whole world praises?" he cried.

"Ah," she answered, "this is not my form. Human eyes can only see me in this state of ugliness, but that you may know what I am like, look in the mirror. It does not let itself be fooled. It will show you my image as it is in truth."

She gave him the mirror in his hand, and in it he saw the most beautiful maiden on earth and saw, too, how the tears were rolling down her cheeks with grief. Then he said, "How can you be set free. I fear no danger."

She answered, "He who gets the crystal ball and holds it before the enchanter will destroy his power with it, and I shall resume my true shape. Ah," she added, "so many have already gone to meet death for this, and you are so young. I fear that you will encounter such great danger."

"Nothing can keep me from doing it," he said, "but tell me what I must do."

"You will know everything," said the king's daughter, "when you descend the mountain on which the castle stands. A wild bull will stand below by a spring, and you must fight with it. And if you have the luck to kill it, a fiery bird will spring out of it, which bears in its body a red-hot egg. In the yolk of the egg lies the crystal ball. The bird, however, will not let the egg fall until forced to do so, and if it falls on the ground, it will flame up and burn everything that is near, and even the egg itself will melt, and with it the crystal ball, and then your trouble will have been in vain."

The youth went down to the spring where the bull snorted and bellowed at him. After a long struggle, he plunged his sword into the animal's body, and it fell down. Instantly, a fiery bird arose from it and was about to fly away, but the young man's brother, the eagle, who was passing between the clouds, swooped down, chased it away to the sea, and struck it with his beak until it let the egg fall. The egg, however, did not fall into the sea, but on a fisherman's hut, which stood on the shore.

The hut began at once to smoke and was about to burst into flames. Then arose in the sea, waves as high as a house, which streamed over the hut and subdued the fire. The other brother, the whale, had come swimming to them and had driven the water up on high.

When the fire was extinguished, the youth searched for the egg and happily found it. It was not yet melted, but the shell was broken by being so suddenly cooled with the water, and he could take out the crystal ball quite easily.

When the youth went to the enchanter and held it before him, the enchanter said, "My power is destroyed, and from this time forth you are the king of the castle of the golden sun. With this you can also give back to your brothers their human form."

Then the youth hurried back to the king's daughter, and when he entered the room, she was standing there in the full splendor of her beauty, and joyfully they exchanged rings with each other and were married. There they lived, happily ever after.

The Owl

TWO OR THREE HUNDRED years ago, when people were far from being so crafty and cunning as they are nowadays, an extraordinary event took place in a little town. By some mischance one of the great owls, called horned owls, had come from the neighboring woods into the barn of one of the townsfolk in the middle of the night. When day broke, the owl did not dare to venture out again from her retreat, for fear of the other birds, which raised a terrible outcry whenever she appeared.

In the morning, when the servant went into the barn to fetch some straw, he was so frightened at the sight of the owl sitting there in the corner, that he ran away and announced to his master that a monster, the likes of which he had never seen in his life, and which could devour a man without the slightest difficulty, was sitting in the barn, rolling its eyes around in its head.

"I know your kind." said the master. "You have enough courage to chase a blackbird around the fields, but when you see a hen lying dead, you have to get a stick before you go near it. I must go and see for myself what kind of a monster it is," added the master. And he went quite boldly into the granary and looked around.

When, however, he saw with his own eyes the strange creature, he was no less terrified than the servant had been. With two leaps he sprang out, ran to his neighbor's house and begged them to help him against an unknown and dangerous beast, or else the whole town might be in danger if it were to break loose out of the barn, where it was shut up.

A great noise and clamor arose in all the streets. The townsmen came armed with spears, hay-forks, knives, and axes, as if they were going out against an enemy. Finally, the senators appeared with the burgomaster at their head. When they had pulled up into the market-place, they marched to the barn and surrounded it on all sides.

At that point, one of the most courageous of them stepped forward and entered with his spear lowered, but came running out immediately afterwards with a shriek and as pale as death. He could not utter a single word.

Two others ventured in next, but they fared no better. At last one stepped foward, a great strong man who was famous for his warlike deeds, and said, "You will not drive away the monster by merely looking at him. We must be serious here, but I see that you have all tuned into scaredy-cats, and not one of you dares to face the animal."

He ordered them to give him some armor, had a sword and spear brought, and armed himself. All praised his courage, though many feared for his life. The two barn-doors were opened, and they saw the owl, which in the meantime had perched herself on the middle of a great cross-beam.

He had a ladder brought, and when he raised it and made ready to climb up, they all cried out to him that he was to bear himself bravely, and commended him to St. George, who slew the dragon. When he had just got to the top, and the owl perceived that he was after her, and was also bewildered by the crowd and the shouting, and knew not how to escape, she rolled her eyes, ruffled her feathers, flapped her wings, snapped her beak, and cried, "Tuwhit, tuwhoo," in a harsh voice.

"Strike home. Strike home." screamed the crowd outside to the valiant hero. Anyone who was standing where I am standing, he said, would not cry, strike home. He certainly did plant his foot one rung higher on the ladder, but then he began to tremble, and half-fainting, went back out again.

Now there was no one left who dared to place himself in such danger. "The monster," they said, "has poisoned and mortally wounded the very strongest man among us, by snapping at him and just breathing on him. Are we, too, to risk our lives?"

They talked about what they should do to prevent the whole town from being destroyed. For a long time everything seemed to be of no use, but at length the burgomaster found an answer. "My opinion," he said, "is that we ought, out of the common purse, to pay for this barn, and whatsoever corn, straw, or hay it contains, and thus indemnify the owner, and then burn down the whole building and the terrible beast with it. That way, no one will have to endanger his life. This is no time for thinking of expense, and stinginess would be ill applied."

All agreed with him. So they set fire to the barn at all four corners, and with it the owl was miserably burned. Let people who will not believe it, go to the town and find out for themselves.

The Moon

ℭ

ONCE UPON A TIME, a long, long time ago, there was a land where the nights were always dark, and the sky spread over it like a black cloth, for there the moon never rose, and no star could shine in the gloom.

At the creation of the world, the light at night had been enough. Three young fellows once went out of this country on a traveling expedition and arrived in another kingdom, where, in the evening when the sun had disappeared behind the mountains, a shining globe was placed on an oak-tree, which shed a soft light far and wide.

With this shining globe, everything could very well be seen and distinguished, even though it was not as bright as the sun. The travelers stopped and asked a countryman who was driving past with his cart, what kind of a light that was. "That is the moon," he answered. "Our mayor bought it for three dollars and fastened it to the oak-tree. He has to pour oil into it daily to keep it clean, so that it may always shine clearly. He receives a dollar a week from us for doing it."

When the countryman had driven away, one of them said, "We could make some use of this lamp. We have an oak-tree at home, which is just as big as this, and we could hang it on that. What a pleasure it would be not to have to feel around at night in the darkness."

"I'll tell you what we'll do," said the second. "We will fetch a cart and horses and carry away the moon. The people here may buy themselves another."

"I'm a good climber," said the third. "I will bring it down."

The fourth brought a cart and horses, and the third climbed the tree, bored a hole in the moon, passed a rope through it, and lowered it down.

When the shining ball lay in the cart, they covered it over with a cloth so that no one would see that they had stolen it. They carried it safely into their own country and placed it on a high oak. Everyone in the country rejoiced when the new lamp let its light shine over the whole land, and bed-rooms and living rooms were filled with its light.

The dwarfs came out of their caves in the rocks, and the tiny elves in their little red coats danced in rings on the meadows. The four took care that the moon was provided with oil, cleaned the wick, and received their weekly dollar. But eventually, they became old men, and when one of them grew ill and saw that he was about to die, he appointed that one quarter of the moon, as his property, should be buried in the grave with him.

When he died, the mayor climbed up the tree and cut off a quarter of the moon with a pair of scissors, and this was placed in his coffin. The light of the moon decreased, but still not visibly.

When the second man died, the second quarter was buried with him, and the light diminished even more. It grew weaker still after the death of the third, who likewise took his part of it away with him. And when the fourth was borne to his grave, the old state of darkness returned to the country. And whenever the people went out at night without their lanterns they knocked their heads together in collision.

When, however, the pieces of the moon had united themselves together again in the world below, where darkness had always prevailed, it came to pass that the dead became restless and awoke from their sleep.

They were astonished when they were able to see again. The moonlight was quite sufficient for them, for their eyes had become so weak that they could not have tolerated the brilliance of the sun.

They rose up and were merry, and fell into their former ways of living. Some of them went to the play and to dance. Others hurried to the public-houses, where they asked for wine, got drunk, brawled, quarreled, and at last took up clubs and hit each other.

The noise became greater and greater, and at last reached even to heaven. St. Peter, who guards the gate of heaven, thought the lower world had broken out in revolt. He got on his horse and rode through the gate of heaven, down into the world below.

There he made the noisy men quiet down, made them lie down in their graves again, took the moon away with him, and hung it up in heaven for all people, in all countries to enjoy.

The Gold Children

ONCE UPON A TIME, there was a poor man and a poor woman who had nothing but a little cottage, and who found their food by fishing, and always lived from hand to mouth. But it came to pass one day when the man was sitting by the water-side and casting his net, that he pulled out a fish made entirely of gold. As he was looking at the fish, full of astonishment, it began to speak and said, "Listen, fisherman, if you will throw me back again into the water, I will change your little hut into a splendid castle."

Then the fisherman answered, "Of what use is a castle to me if I have nothing to eat?"

The gold fish continued, "That shall be taken care of. There will be a cupboard in the castle in which, when you open it, will have dishes covered with the most delicate meats, and as many of them as you can desire."

"If that be true," said the man, "then I can sure do you the favor."

"Yes," said the fish. "There is, however, the condition that you shall disclose to no one in the world, whoever he may be, where your good luck came from. If you speak even one single word, all will be over."

Then the man threw the wonderful fish back again into the water, and went home. When he arrived, he saw that were his old hut had formerly stood, now stood a great castle. He opened his eyes wide, entered, and saw his wife dressed in beautiful clothes, sitting in a splendid room, and she was quite delighted. She said, "Husband, how has all this come to pass? It suits me very well."

"Yes," said the man, "it suits me too, but I am frightfully hungry, just give me something to eat."

The wife answered, "But I have nothing to feed you and don't know where to find anything in this new house."

"You don't need to know," said the man, "for I believe there will be food that great cupboard. You only need to unlock it."

When she opened it, there stood cakes, meat, fruit, wine, quite a bright prospect. Then the woman cried joyfully, "What more can you want, my dear." And they sat down, and ate and drank together.

When they had had enough, the woman said, "But husband, where did all of this come from?"

"Alas," he answered. "Do not question me about it, for I cannot tell you anything. If I tell anyone, then all our good fortune will disappear."

"Very good," she said. "If I am not to know anything, then I do not want to know anything."

However, she did not really mean what she said. She never rested day or night, and she goaded her husband until in his impatience he revealed that all was owing to a wonderful golden fish which he had caught, and to which in return he had given its liberty. And as soon as the secret was out, the splendid castle with the cupboard immediately disappeared. They were once more in the old fisherman's hut, and the man was obliged to follow his former trade and fish.

But fortune would so have it, that he once more pulled out the golden fish. "Listen," said the fish. "If you will throw me back into the water again, I will once more give you the castle with the cupboard full of roast and boiled meats. Only be firm, for your life's sake, don't tell anyone how you got it, or you will lose it all again."

"I will take good care," answered the fisherman. And he threw the fish back into the water. Back at home everything was once more in its former magnificence, and the wife was overjoyed at their good fortune. But curiosity left her no peace, so that after a couple of days she began to ask again how it had come to pass, and how he had managed to secure it. The man kept silent for a short time, but at last, she made him so angry that he broke out and betrayed the secret.

In an instant, the castle disappeared and they were back again in their old hut. "Now you have got what you want," he said, "and we can gnaw at a bare bone again."

"Ah," said the woman, "I would rather not have riches if I cannot know from where they come, for then I have no peace."

The man went back to fish, and after awhile he chanced to pull out the gold fish for a third time. "Listen," said the fish, "I see very well that I am fated to fall into your hands. Take me home and cut me into six pieces. Give your wife two of them to eat, two to your horse, and bury two of them in the ground. Then they will bring you a blessing."

The fisherman took the fish home with him, and did as it had instructed him. It came to pass, however, that from the two pieces that were buried in the ground two golden lilies sprang up; the horse had two golden foals, and the fisherman's wife bore two children who were made entirely of gold.

The children grew up, became tall and handsome, and the lilies and horses did too. One day, the children said, "Father, we want to ride our golden horses and travel out in the world."

But he answered sorrowfully, "How will I bear it if you go away, and I know not what happens to you?"

Then they said, "The two golden lilies remain here. Through them you can see how it is with us. If they are fresh, then we are in health. If they are withered, we are ill. If they perish, then we are dead."

So they rode away and came to an inn, in which were many people. When all the people saw the gold children, they began to laugh and make fun of them. When one of them heard the mocking, he felt ashamed and would not go out into the world, but turned back and went home again to his father. But the other child rode forward and reached a great forest. As he was about to enter it, the people said, "It is not safe for you to ride through. The wood is full of robbers who would treat you badly. You have bad luck. When the robbers see that you are made of gold, and your horse is too, they will kill you for sure."

But he would not allow himself to be frightened, and said, "I must and will ride through it." Then he took bear-skins and covered himself and his horse with them, so that the gold could not be seen. He rode fearlessly into the forest. When he had ridden onward a little, he heard a rustling in the bushes and heard voices speaking together. From one side came cries of, "There is one, but from the other, let him go. It is a bearskin, as poor and bare as a church-mouse. We have nothing to gain from him." So the gold-child rode joyfully through the forest, and nothing bad happened to him.

One day he entered a village where he saw a maiden, who was so beautiful that he did not believed she must be the most beautiful maiden in the whole world. And as such a mighty love took possession of him. He went up to her and said, "I love you with my whole heart, will you be my wife?"

He, too, pleased the maiden so much that she agreed and said, "Yes, I will be your wife, and be true to you my whole life long."

Then they were married, and just as they were in the greatest happiness, the father of the bride came home. When he saw that his daughter's wedding was being celebrated, he was astonished, and said, "Where is the bridegroom?"

They showed him the gold-child, who, however, still wore his bear-skins. To this, the father said wrathfully, "A bearskin shall never marry my daughter," and was about to kill him.

The bride begged as hard as she could and said, "He is my husband, and I love him with all my heart."

Finally the father gave in. Nevertheless, the idea never left his thoughts. So that next morning he rose early, wishing to see whether his daughter's husband was a common ragged beggar. But when he peeped in, he saw a magnificent golden man in the bed, and the bear-skins lying on the ground. He went back to his room and thought, "What a good thing it was that I restrained my anger. I would have committed a great crime."

But the gold-child dreamed that he rode out to hunt a splendid stag, and when he awoke in the morning, he said to his wife, "I must go out hunting."

She was uneasy, and begged him to stay there, and said, "You might easily meet with a great misfortune."

But he answered, "I must go and I will."

He got up and rode into the forest, and it was not long before a fine stag crossed his path exactly according to his dream. He aimed and was about to shoot it, when the stag ran away. He chased it over hedges and ditches the whole day without feeling tired, but in the evening, the stag vanished from his sight. When the gold-child looked around him, he noticed that he was standing in front of a little house, where a witch sat inside.

He knocked and a little old woman came out and asked, "What are you doing so late in the midst of the great forest?"

"Have you seen a stag? he asked.

"Yes," she answered. "I know the stag well." At that moment, a little dog which had come out of the house with her, barked at the man violently.

"Will you be silent, you odious toad," he said, "or I will shoot you dead."

Then the witch cried out in a passion, "You will not slay my little dog!" And immediately, she transformed him, so that he lay like a stone, and his bride waited for him in vain and thought, "That which I so greatly dreaded, which lay so heavily on my heart, has come upon him."

But at home, the other brother was standing by the gold-lilies, when one of them suddenly drooped. "Good heavens," he said. "My brother has met with some great misfortune. I must away to see if I can possibly rescue him."

Then the father said, "Stay here. If I lose you also, what shall I do?"

But he answered, "I must and will go look for my brother."

Then he mounted his golden horse, and rode out and entered the great forest, where his brother lay turned to stone.

The old witch came out of her house and called him, wishing to entrap him also. But he did not go near her, and said, "I will shoot you, if you will not bring my brother to life again."

She touched the stone, though very unwillingly, with her forefinger, and he was immediately restored to his human shape. And the two gold-children rejoiced when they saw each other again, kissed and hugged each other, and rode away together out of the forest. One home to his bride, and the other to his father.

The father then said, "I knew well that you had rescued your brother, for the golden lily suddenly rose up and blossomed out again. Then they lived happily for the rest of their lives.

Jorinda and Joringel

⌘

THERE WAS ONCE an old castle in the midst of a large and dense forest. In it lived an old woman who was a witch who was all alone. In the daytime she changed herself into a car or an owl, but in the evening she took her proper shape again as a human witch.

She could lure wild beasts and birds to her, and then she killed and boiled and roasted them. If anyone came within one hundred paces of her castle, the person had to stand still, and could not move from the place until she set him free.

Whenever an innocent maiden came within this circle, she changed the maiden into a bird and locked her up in a wicker-bird cage, and carried the cage into a room in the castle. She had about seven thousand cages of rare birds in the castle.

Now, there was once a maiden who was called Jorinda, who was prettier than all other girls. She and a handsome youth named Joringel had promised to marry each other. They were not yet married, but engaged to be, and their greatest happiness was being together.

One day, in order that they would be able to talk together in peace, they went for a walk in the forest. "Take care," said Joringel, "that you do not go too near the castle."

It was a beautiful evening. The sun shone brightly between the trunks of the trees into the dark green of the forest, and the turtle-doves sang mournfully from the trees. Jorinda wept now and then. She sat down in the sunshine and was sorrowful. Joringel was sorrowful too. They were as sad as if they were about to die.

Then they looked around them, and were quite at a loss, for they did not know the way to get back home. The sun was still half above the mountain and half under. Joringel looked through the bushes and saw the old walls of the castle close at hand. He was horror-stricken and filled with deadly fear.

Jorinda was singing, "my little bird, with the necklace red, sings sorrow, sorrow, sorrow, he sings that the dove must soon be dead, sings sorrow, sor - jug, jug, jug."

Joringel looked for Jorinda. She had been changed into a nightingale, and sang, "jug, jug, jug." A screech-owl with glowing eyes flew three times around about her, and three times cried, "to-whoo, to-whoo, to-whoo."

Joringel could not move. He stood there like a stone and could neither weep nor speak, nor move his hands or feet. The sun had now set. The owl flew into the thicket, and directly afterwards there came out of it a crooked old woman, yellow and lean, with large red eyes and a hooked nose, the point of which reached to her chin.

She muttered to herself, caught the nightingale, and took it away in her hand. Joringel could neither speak nor move from the spot. The nightingale was gone. At last, the woman came back, and said in a hollow voice,"Greet you, Zachiel. If the moon shines on the cage, Zachiel, let him loose at once." Suddenly, Joringel was freed. He fell on his knees before the woman and begged her to give him back his Jorinda. But she said that he would never see her again, and then she went away. He called, he cried, he lamented, but all in vain, "What ever will I do without my Jorinda."

Joringel went away, and at last came to a strange village, where he took a job caring for sheep. He often walked around and around the castle where the witch lived, but he never got too close. At last, he dreamed one night that he found a blood-red flower, in the middle of which was a beautiful large pearl. In the dream, he picked the flower and went with it to the castle, and everything he touched with the flower was freed from witch's enchantment. He also dreamed that with the flower, he was able to save Jorinda.

In the morning, when he awoke, he began to look everywhere for such a flower. He looked every day for nine days, and then, early in the morning, he found the blood-red flower. In the middle of it was a large dew-drop, as big as the finest pearl. Day and night he journeyed with this flower to the castle.

When he was within a hundred paces of it he was not frozen and turned to stone, but instead, he was able to walk up to the door. Joringel was full of joy. He touched the door with the flower and it sprang open. He walked in through the courtyard and listened for the sound of the birds. At last he heard it. He went in and found the room from where the birds were singing, and there the witch was feeding the birds in the seven thousand cages.

When the witch saw Joringel she was angry, very angry, and scolded and spat poison and gall at him, but she could not come within two paces of him. He did not take any notice of her, but went and looked at the cages with the birds. But there were many hundred nightingales, how was he to find his Jorinda again. Just then, he saw the old woman quietly take away a cage with a bird in it, and go towards the door. Swiftly he sprang towards her, touched the cage with the flower, and also the old woman.

She could now no longer bewitch anyone. And Jorinda was standing there, clasping him around the neck, and she was as beautiful as ever. Then all the other birds were turned into maidens again, and he went home with his Jorinda, and they lived happily together for a long, long time.

The True Sweetheart

♥

THERE WAS ONCE upon a time a girl who was young and beautiful, but she had lost her mother when she was only a small child, and her step-mother did all she could to make the girl's life miserable.

Whenever this woman gave her any chores to do, she worked at it very hard, and did everything that lay in her power. Still she could not touch the heart of the wicked woman. She was never satisfied, it was never enough. The harder the girl worked, the more chores the step-mother gave her, and all that the woman thought of was how to weigh her down with still heavier burdens, and make her life still more miserable.

One day the step-mother said to her, "Here are twelve pounds of feathers which you must pick, and if they are not done this evening, you may expect a good beating. Do you imagine you are to idle away the whole day?"

The poor girl sat down to do the work, but tears ran down her cheeks as she did so, for she saw plainly enough that it was quite impossible to finish the work in one day. Whenever she had a little heap of feathers lying before her, and she sighed or clapped her hands together in her anguish, the feathers flew away, and she had to pick them up again, and begin her work anew.

After a long while, she put her elbows on the table, laid her face in her two hands, and cried, "Is there no one, then, on God's earth to have pity on me?"

Then she heard a low voice which said, "Be comforted, my child. I have come to help you."

The maiden looked up, and an old woman was by her side. She took the girl kindly by the hand, and said, "Only tell me what is troubling you."

As she spoke so kindly, the girl told her of her miserable life, and how one burden after another was laid upon her, and she never could get to the end of the work which was given to her. "If I have don't have these feathers ready by this evening, my step-mother will beat me, she has threatened she will, and I know she keeps her word."

Her tears began to flow again, but the good old woman said, "Do not be afraid, my child. Rest a while, and in the meantime I will look to your work. The girl lay down on her bed, and soon fell asleep. The old woman seated herself at the table with the feathers, and how they did fly off the quills, which she scarcely touched with her withered hands. The twelve pounds were soon finished, and when the girl awoke, great heaps of feathers were lying, piled up, and everything in the room was neatly cleared away, but the old woman had vanished.

The maiden thanked God, and sat still until evening came. When the step-mother came in and marveled to see the work completed. "Just look, you awkward creature," she said, "what can be done when people are industrious, and why could you not set about something else. There you sit with your hands crossed."

When she went out she said, "The creature is worth more than her salt. I must give her some more work that is harder. The next morning she called the girl, and said, "There is a spoon for you. Using only this spoon, you must empty out the great pond which is beside the garden, and if it is not done by night, you know what will happen."

The girl took the spoon, and saw that it was full of holes, but even if it had not been, she never could have emptied the pond with it. She set to work at once, knelt down by the water, into which her tears were falling, and began to empty it. But the good old woman appeared again, and when she learned about what the mean stepmother was demanding, she said, "Be of good cheer, my child. Go into the thicket and lie down and sleep. I will do your work."

As soon as the old woman was alone, she barely touched the pond, and a vapor rose up from the water and mingled itself with the clouds. Gradually the pond was emptied, and when the maiden awoke before sunset and came to see the pond, she saw nothing but the fishes which were struggling in the mud. She went to her step-mother, and showed her that the work was done.

"It ought to have been done long before this," she said, and grew white with anger, but she meditated something new.

On the third morning she said to the girl, "You must build me a castle on the plain there, and it must be ready by the evening."

The maiden was dismayed, and said, "How can I possibly complete such a difficult task?"

"I will endure no opposition, screamed the step-mother. If you can empty a pond with a spoon that is full of holes, you can build a castle too. I will move into it this very day, and if anything is wrong with it, even if it be the most trifling thing in the kitchen or cellar, you know what lies before you."

She drove the girl out, and when she entered the valley, the rocks were there, piled up one above the other, and all her strength would not have enabled her even to move the very smallest of them. She sat down and wept, and still she hoped the old woman would help her. The old woman soon appeared. She comforted her and said, "Lie down there in the shade and sleep, and I will soon build the castle for you. If you want, you can live in it yourself."

When the maiden had gone away, the old woman touched the gray rocks. They began to rise, moved together, and stood there as if giants had built the walls. And on these walls, the building arose and it seemed as if countless hands were working invisibly, and placing one stone upon another. There was a dull heavy noise from the ground, pillars arose all by themselves and placed themselves in order near each other.

The tiles laid themselves in order on the roof, and when noon-day came, the great weather-cock was already turning itself on the summit of the tower, like a golden maid with fluttering garments. The inside of the castle was being finished while evening was drawing near.

How the old woman managed it, no one knows, but the walls of the rooms were hung with silk and velvet, embroidered chairs were there, and richly ornamented arm-chairs by marble tables, crystal chandeliers hung down from the ceilings, and mirrored themselves in the smooth floor, green parrots were there in gilt cages, and so were strange birds which sang most beautifully. Everywhere you could see was as much magnificence as if a king were going to live there.

The sun was just setting when the girl awoke, and the brightness of a thousand lights flashed in her face. She hurried to the castle, and entered by the open door. The steps were spread with red cloth, and the golden railing was covered with flowering trees. When she saw the splendor of the rooms, she stood as if turned to stone. Who knows how long she might have stood there if she had not remembered the step-mother.

"Alas," she said to herself, "if only my step-mother could but be satisfied at last, and would stop trying to make my life a misery."

The girl went and told her step-mother that the castle was ready. "I will move into it at once," said she, and rose from her seat. When they entered the castle, she was forced to hold her hand before her eyes, the brilliancy of everything was so dazzling. "You see," she said to the girl, "how easy it has been for you to do this. I should have given you something harder."

She went through all the rooms, and examined every corner to see if anything was wrong or defective, but she could discover nothing. "Now we will go down below," she said, looking at the girl with malicious eyes. "The kitchen and the cellar still have to be examined, and if you have forgotten anything you shall not escape your punishment."

They went downstairs to find that a fire was burning on the hearth, and the meat was cooking in the pans, the tongs and shovel were leaning against the wall, and the shining brazen utensils all arranged in sight. Nothing was missing, not even a coal-box and a water-pail.

"Which is the way to the cellar," she cried. "If it is not abundantly filled with wine bottles, you will be in big trouble." She raised up the trap-door and descended, but she had hardly made two steps before the heavy trap-door, which was only laid back, fell down. The girl heard a scream, lifted up the door very quickly to go to her aid, but she had fallen down, and the girl found her lying lifeless at the bottom.

Now the magnificent castle belonged to the girl alone. At first, she could not believe it was true. Beautiful dresses were hanging in the closets, the chests were filled with gold and silver, or with pearls and jewels, and she never felt a desire that she was not able to gratify.

And soon the fame of the beauty and riches of the maiden was told all over the world. Wooers presented themselves daily but none pleased her. At length, the son of the king came and he knew how to touch her heart, and she agreed to marry him.

In the garden of the castle was a lime-tree, under which they were one day sitting together, when he said to her, "I will go home and obtain my father's consent to our marriage. I trust you to wait for me under this lime-tree. I shall be back in a few hours."

The maiden kissed him on his left cheek, and said, "Be true to me, and never let anyone else kiss you on this cheek. I will wait here under the lime-tree until you return."

The maid stayed beneath the lime-tree until sunset, but her prince did not return. She sat for three days from morning to evening, waiting for him, but in vain. As he still was not there by the fourth day, she said, "Some accident must have happened. I will go out and look for him, and will not come back until I have found him."

She packed up three of her most beautiful dresses, one embroidered with bright stars, the second with silver moons, the third with golden suns, tied up a handful of jewels in her handkerchief, and set out. She asked people everywhere for her prince, but no one had seen him, no one knew anything about him.

Far and wide did she wander through the world, but she could not find him. At last, she had to get a job with a farmer as a cowherd. She buried her dresses and jewels beneath a stone, and now she lived as a herdswoman, guarded her herd, and was very sad and full of longing for her beloved prince.

She had a little baby calf that she taught to know her, and fed it out of her own hand. One day she said, "Little calf, little calf, kneel by my side, and do not forget your cowherd-maid, as the prince forgot his betrothed bride, who waited for him beneath the lime-tree's shade."

The little calf knelt down, and she stroked it on the head. And when she had lived for a couple of years alone and full of grief, a report was spread over all the land that the king's daughter was about to celebrate her marriage. The road to the town passed through the village where the maiden was living, and it came to pass that once when the maiden was driving out her herd, the prince traveled by.

He was sitting proudly on his horse and never looked around, but when she saw him she recognized her beloved prince, and it was just as if a sharp knife had pierced her heart. "Alas," she said, "I believed him true to me, but he has forgotten me."

The next day he again came along the road. When he was near her she said to the little calf, "Little calf, little calf, kneel by my side, and do not forget your cowherd-maid, as the prince forgot his betrothed bride, who waited for him beneath the lime-tree's shade."

When he heard her voice, he looked down and reined in his horse. He looked into the girl's face and then put his hands before his eyes as if he were trying to remember something, but he soon rode onwards and was out of sight.

"Alas," she said, "he no longer knows me."

And her grief was ever greater. Soon after this a great festival three days long was to be held at the king's court, and the whole country was invited to it.

"Now will I try my last chance," thought the maiden, and when evening came she went to the stone under which she had buried her treasures. She took out the dress with the golden suns, put it on, and adorned herself with the jewels. She let down her hair, which she had concealed under a handkerchief, and it fell down in long curls around her, and thus she went into the town, and in the darkness no one noticed her.

When she entered the brightly lighted hall, everyone started back in amazement, but no one knew who she was. The king's son went to meet her, but he did not recognize her. He led her out to dance, and was so enchanted with her beauty, that he thought no more of the other bride. When the feast was over, she vanished in the crowd, and hurried back to the village, where she once more put on her herd's dress.

The next evening she took out the dress with the silver moons, and put a half-moon made of precious stones in her hair. When she appeared at the festival, all eyes were turned upon her, but the king's son rushed to meet her, and filled with love for her, danced with her alone, and no longer so much as glanced at anyone else. Before she went away he made her promise to come again to the festival on the next evening.

When she appeared for the third time, she wore the star-dress which sparkled at every step she took, and her hair-ribbon and girdle were starred with jewels. The prince had already been waiting for her for a long time, and forced his way up to her. "Do but tell who you are," he said. "I feel just as if I had already known you a long time."

"Do you not know what I did when you left me?" Then she stepped up to him, and kissed him on his left cheek, and in a moment it was as if scales fell from his eyes, and he recognized his true bride.

"Come," he said to her, "here I stay no longer." He gave her his hand and led her down to the carriage. The horses hurried away to the magic castle as if the wind had been harnessed to the carriage. The illuminated windows already shone in the distance. When they drove past the lime-tree, countless glow-worms were swarming about it. It shook its branches, and sent forth their fragrance.

On the steps of the magic castle, flowers were blooming, and the room echoed with the song of strange birds, but in the hall the entire court was assembled, and the priest was waiting to marry the prince and the true bride.

Frederick & Catherine

ONCE UPON A TIME, there was a man who was called Frederick and a woman called Catherine, who had married each other and lived together as young married folks. One day Frederick said, "I will now go and plough. Catherine, when I come back, there must be some roast meat on the table for my hunger, and a fresh drink for my thirst."

"Just go, Frederick," answered Catherine. "Just go. I will have everything ready for you when you return."

So when dinner-time drew near she got a sausage out of the chimney, put it in the frying-pan, put some butter to it, and fired up the stove. The sausage began to fry and to hiss. Catherine stood beside it and held the handle of the pan, and had her own thoughts as she was doing it.

Then it occurred to her, "While the sausage is getting done you could go into the cellar and get the beer."

So she set the frying-pan safely on the fire, took a can, and went down into the cellar to pour some beer. The beer ran into the can and she watched it. Then she thought, "Oh, dear. The dog upstairs is not fastened up, it might get the sausage out of the pan. Lucky I thought of it." And in a snap she was up the cellar-steps again, but she was too late. The dog had the sausage in its mouth already, and trailed it away on the ground.

Catherine, who was not lazy, set out after the dog. She chased it a long way into the field. The dog, however, was faster than Catherine and did not let the sausage go, but skipped over the furrows with it. "What's gone is gone," she said, and turned around. Because she had run until she was tired, she walked quietly and comfortably, and cooled herself.

During this time, the beer was still running out of the cask, for she had not turned off the tap. And when the can was full and there was no other place for it, it ran into the cellar and did not stop until the whole cask was empty. As soon as she was on the steps she saw the accident.

"Good gracious," she cried. "What will I do now to stop Frederick finding out?" She thought for a while, and at last she remembered that up in the attic was a sack of the finest wheat flour from the last fair, and she would get that down and throw it over the beer.

"Yes," she said, "he who saves a thing when he should, has it afterwards when he needs it, and she climbed up to the garret and carried the sack below, and threw it straight down on the can of beer, which she knocked over, and Frederick's drink was also spilled.

"It is all right," said Catherine. "I will cover this the way I covered the other." And she tossed the flour over the whole cellar. When it was done she was heartily delighted with her work, and said, "How clean and wholesome it does look here."

At mid-day, Frederick came home. "Oh, lovely wife, what did you make me for dinner?"

"Ah, Frederick," she answered, "I was frying a sausage for you, but while I was pouring you a beer to drink with it, the dog grabbed it out of the pan. And while I was running after the dog, all the beer ran out, and while I was drying up the beer with the flour, I knocked over your glass as well, but don't worry, the cellar is quite dry again."

"Catherine. Catherine, you should not have done that, to let the sausage be carried off and the beer run out of the cask, and throw out all our flour at the same time."

"Well, Frederick, I did not know that. You should have told me before this all happened."

The man thought, "If this is the kind of wife I have, I had better take more care of things." Now he had saved up a good number of dollars, which he changed into gold, and said to Catherine, "Look, these are yellow counters for playing games, I will put them in a pot and bury them in the stable under the cow's manger, but you need to stay away from them and leave them alone."

She said, "Oh, no, Frederick, I certainly will not go near them."

One day, when Frederick was gone some pedlars came into the village who had cheap clay bowls and pots, and asked the young woman if there was anything she wanted to buy. "Oh, dear people, said Catherine, I have no money and can buy nothing, but if you have any use for yellow counters I will buy something from you."

"Yellow counters, why not. But just let us see them."

"Sure. Just go into the stable and dig under the cow's manger, and you will find the yellow counters. I am not allowed to go there."

The rogues went to the manger, dug underneath it, and found pure gold. Then they gathered it all up, ran away, and left their pots and bowls behind in the house.

Catherine wanted to use her new pots, but she did not need anything more in the kitchen. So she decided to knock the bottom out of every pot, and set them all as ornaments on the fence that went around about the house.

When Frederick came and saw the new decorations, he said, "Catherine, where did these decorations come from?"

"I bought them, Frederick, with the yellow game counters that were under the cow's manger. Don't' worry, I did not go there myself. The pedlars had to dig them out on their own."

"Ah, wife," said Frederick, "what have you done. Those were not counters, but pure gold and all our wealth. You should not have done that."

"Indeed, Frederick," she said, "I did not know that they were gold coins. You told me they were game counters." Catherine stood for awhile and wondered, then she said, "Listen, Frederick, we will soon get the gold back again. We will run after the thieves."

"Come, then." said Frederick. "We will try it, but bring some butter and cheese so that we will have something to eat on the way."

"Yes, Frederick, I will take them."

They set out, and as Frederick was the better walker, Catherine followed him. "It is to my advantage." she thought, "When we turn back I will be a little way in advance."

Soon they came to a hill where there were deep ruts on both sides of the road. "Here you can see," said Catherine, "how they have torn and skinned and galled the poor earth. It will never be whole again as long as it lives." And in her heart's compassion, she took her butter and smeared the ruts right and left, so they would not be so hurt by the wheels, and as she was bending down in her charity, one of the cheeses rolled out of her pocket down the hill.

"I already climbed up here once," said Catherine. "I will not go down again. I will send another cheese to run and fetch it back." So she took another cheese and rolled it down the hill. But the cheeses did not come back, so she let a third run down, thinking, "Perhaps they are waiting for company, and do not like to walk alone."

When none of the cheese returned, she said, "I do not know what that can mean, but it may perhaps be that the third has not found the way, and has gotten lost. I will just send the fourth to call it." But the fourth did no better than the third. This made Catherine angry, and she threw down the fifth and sixth as well, and these were her last pieces of cheese.

She remained standing for some time watching for their coming, but when they still did not come, she said, "Oh, you are terrible cheeses. I didn't want to eat you anyway. Do you think I will wait any longer for you? I shall go my way, and you can run after me, you have younger legs than I."

Catherine went on and found Frederick, who was standing waiting for her because he wanted something to eat. "Let's us have a bite to eat. What you have brought for us?"

She gave him the dry bread. "Where is the butter and where are the cheeses?" asked the man.

"Ah, Frederick," said Catherine, "I smeared the cart-ruts with the butter and the cheeses will come soon, one ran away from me, so I sent the others after to call it."

"You should not have done that, Catherine, to smear the butter on the road and let the cheeses run down the hill. Now we have nothing to eat but dry bread."

"Really, Frederick, you should have told me."

Then they ate the dry bread together, and Frederick said, "Catherine, did you lock the door when you left the house?"

"No, Frederick, you should have told me to do it before."

"Then go home again, and lock up the house before we go any farther, and bring with you something else for us to eat. I will wait here for you."

Catherine went back and thought, "Frederick wants something more to eat. He does not like butter and cheese, so I will take with me a handkerchief full of dried pears and a pitcher of vinegar for him to drink."

Then she locked the front door, but unhinged the back door to bring with her, believing that when she had locked the front door, the house would be secure. Catherine took her time on the way, and thought, "Frederick will rest himself so much the longer."

When she had once reached him she said, "Here is the back door for you, Frederick, and now you can take care of the house yourself."

"Oh, heavens," he said. "What a strange wife I have. She takes the back door off the hinges so that everyone and everything may run into the house, and locks the front door." He said to her, "It is now too late to go back home again, but since you have brought the door here, you will have to carry it."

"I will carry the door, Frederick, but the dried pears and the vinegar-jug will be too heavy for me. I will hang them on the door and it will carry them."

They went into the forest and sought the rogues who had stolen the coins, but they could not find them. As night came and it grew dark, they climbed into a tree and decided to spend the night there. As soon as they sat down, the thieves appeared. They sat down under the very tree in which Frederick and Catherine were sitting, lighted a fire, and were about to divide their booty.

Frederick got down on the other side and collected some stones. Then he climbed up with them so he could throw them at the thieves and kill them. The stones, however, did not hit them, and the thieves soon announced, "Morning must be near; the wind is shaking down the fir-cones on us."

Catherine still had the door on her back, and as it pressed so heavily on her, she thought it was the fault of the dried pears, and said, "Frederick, I must throw the pears down."

"No, Catherine, not now," he replied. "The thieves will see us hiding up here."

"Oh, but, Frederick, I must. They weigh me down far too much."

"Do it, then, and you will pay the price for it."

She dropped dried pears and they rolled down between the branches, and the thieves below said, "Those are birds, droppings."

A short time afterwards, as the door was still heavy, Catherine said, "Ah, Frederick, I must pour out the vinegar."

"No, Catherine, you must not, they might see us."

"Ah, but, Frederick, I must. It weighs me down far too much. Then do it and you will pay the price for it."

So she emptied out the vinegar, and it spattered over the robbers. They said amongst themselves, "The dew is already falling."

At length Catherine thought, "Can it really be the door that weighs me down so much?" She said, "Frederick, I must throw the door down."

"No, not now, Catherine, they might see us."

"Oh, but, Frederick, I must. It weighs me down far too much."

"Oh, no, Catherine, hold on to it."

"Ah, Frederick, I am letting it fall."

"Let it go, then, in the devil's name."

Then it fell down with a violent clatter, and the thieves below cried, "The devil is coming down the tree, and they ran away and left everything behind them, even the coins.

Early the next morning, when the two came down they found all their gold again and carried it home.

The Complete Grimm's Fairy Tales

The End

Printed in Great Britain
by Amazon